THE SPOT OF LIFE

AUSTIN HALL

THE SPOT OF LIFE

Originally published in 1932 as a serial
in Argosy Weekly.

ISBN 13: 978-1-4344-8564-9

THE SPOT OF LIFE

Ｌ𝐄𝐓 us go back and examine the facts as we encountered them on that day in November—the day that marked the reopening of the Blind Spot.

The Blind Spot!

It had become merely a memory—one of those fascinating mysteries that are washed in legend. But suddenly it had come back, potent with menace—and threatening destruction. Some called it the Occult; but in the light of what happened during those memorable days we have learned a lot. Most of all, we must thank the firmness and courage of Halbert Watson, son of a famous father, and the peculiar run of circumstance that led him into the great Unknown!

I

THE BAR SENESTRO

THE SATURDAY before Thanksgiving is ever a festive day in California, for it is on that date that the classic of Western football is pulled off—the big game—Stanford vs. California. A day of days—distinctive not only for its sports, but for its weather. We do not know why; but it is a fact that the weather is proverbial; very little wind, medium temperature, sometimes a fog in the morning, but always clearing away for the glorious afternoon.

We know two things about that particular morning: first, it was foggy; secondly, most everyone in San Francisco was wearing colors—red, or blue and gold, according to their favorites. A mist was slithering down the length of Market Street, gray and obscuring. Business was just so so; the game was the thing!

Remember it was a foggy morning!

Perhaps this is the reason why no one noticed the man until he reached Market Street. Be that as it may, he was first observed close by Third Street, where he stopped to purchase a paper, stepping nonchalantly to the newsstand. Two men were working at the corner. One of them heard a voice, picked a coin from the outstretched hand, and glanced up.

"Hey," he exclaimed suddenly. "Hey! Yessir! You buy paper? Thank you, sir."

Tony Moreno knew types; but the one in front of him was different—like an apparition. Almost immediately that notion passed away, and suddenly the man became a cross between a Stanford undergraduate and a movie star. Tony Moreno was not the one to analyze reactions. Here was a tall man, possibly six feet two inches, broad shouldered, handsome; clad in vestments never before seen along Market Street—a sort of tunic woven from a feathery-like fabric, bright red, caught over one shoulder, leaving the left arm bare.

A strange man!

He smiled at Tony's words; then suddenly there came a peculiar transition; the lips hardened, his features shifted, with a sort of deadening effect. We have the words of Tony Moreno.

"One look and he would kill you. I was 'fraid of dat man."

And there were others. In the light of what was to follow each detail is important. We had forgotten the original mystery; so we were doubly mystified. But as to the man's personal appearance, all are agreed. Certainly he was handsome and kingly. But no one ever dreamed that he was a king in fact.

It is a strange story.

The newcomer turned slowly into Market Street and from that moment he became the center of tremendous interest. Men looked and wondered, nodded their heads, and classified him as some student connected with the Stanford rooting section.

Certainly they never dreamed of what he was.

Why should they?

10

THE SPOT OF LIFE

But not so the women. The fair sex looked and wondered. Here was a man with everything—romance, glamour, figure, poise. It is not surprising that the witnesses who later testified were mostly of the feminine gender. Yet there was one other.

We refer to Detective Samuel J. Flanning. And we are thankful for the circumstance that guided him to that section of Market Street and the fact that, like another detective many years before, he chanced to run into the mystery just as it was breaking.

However, the detective knew nothing about that. He was merely taking a day off, and, with a big game ticket in his pocket, was heading for the stadium over in Berkeley. Certainly he had no inkling that the greatest moment of his life was approaching, in fact, had arrived.

Perhaps it was just fate.

Be that as it may, the two men came together. A crowd had gathered around the stranger and was escorting him down Market Street. The detective was curious; he worked his way into the midst of the jam. Two girls were laughing; one spoke out.

"Gee, Mame! Ain't he the sweetest thing? Some movie star, I bet."

And that was about the sum total of the officer's conclusion. But just then the stranger glanced over the crowd with a sort of royal hopelessness. The officer smiled. Something urged him forward. It was an act of impulse, but of tremendous significance.

The stranger was unusual, fascinating. Surely, Destiny was working. The detective spoke:

"Heading for the Ferry?"

It was a chance question; the crowd had divided; the

11

stranger stopped suddenly, turned. The detective thrust out his hand.

"Why, yes," came the slowly articulated words, "the Ferry? Did you say the Ferry? Let me see now!"

The man stopped, opened the feathery tunic, revealing an inner garment of silvery sheen, thrust his finger into a pocket, and brought out a wrinkled parchment, smoothed it upon his palm and held it out to the detective. What could the fellow mean? The detective drew his interrogator to the shelter of a doorway, spread the paper in his hand.

It was puzzling.

The parchment was very old—like one rummaged from a pyramid; the markings were still stranger. At first glance it looked like a bill head—with the outlines of a city engraved at the crest, a city of bubbling pagodas and palaces, splashed with hieroglyphics. But stranger than all was a map, that of lower San Francisco. A straight line and arrows indicated the direction toward the Ferry.

"You mean," asked the detective, "that you are going to Berkeley? I suppose you're heading for the big game like everybody else? What's the big idea?"

He tapped the paper and looked at his companion. Here undoubtedly was a student pulling off some masterpiece of fun. But it was a college day; the detective was lenient. The youth was a good actor. He opened his lips, spoke in a mellow tone—strange words—such as might have come from the language of dreams.

"Ah, yes, to be sure. The game? I have heard of that too. I might have known. For was not his lordship Chick Watson of a mighty sort—a great man given to feats of strength—worthy indeed of a Senestro? But I am told he has a son, a younger man. His name?"

Here is another curious hookup. Let us pause to consider. The captain of the California varsity on this particular after-

12

noon was none other than Hal Watson, son of an illustrious father, the famous Chick Watson of an older day. Fortunately, the detective was slightly past middle age; the mention of a hero of his boyhood called up a picture.

His thoughts raced back to the time when the man who now held the chair of philosophy at the University of California was racing to a touchdown. It was a far cry, to be sure. Then as suddenly he came back to the present—now there was another Watson, a son named Hal to perpetuate the glory of the father. Everybody in the country knew all about it; the papers were full. So it couldn't be anything but trickery.

"You mean that you are going to Berkeley?" he sparred. "And that you wish to see Hal Watson?"

"That's it," spoke the other. "A youth named Hal Watson. He lived on Dwight Way."

Surely we can't blame Detective Samuel J. Flanning. He glanced out at the moving multitude; everybody was rushing for the boat. Each moment added to the excitement.

So why not? Here was another hoax tuned to the music of the Great American Band Wagon. He wondered what it could be. But such is youth! The detective sighed.

"All right," he spoke with a smile, "I'm biting. We'll hail a taxi. By the way, that make-up you have on is a beaut. You look like a man from Mars."

The stranger smiled. Once again he answered in that modulated tone:

"A man from Mars? I do not understand, sir. But I come from a far country. Yes, indeed!"

13

II

A STRANGE MEETING!

TEN MINUTES later a gray taxicab deposited its contents at the Ferry Building. The chauffeur nodded at the detective.

"Stanford, eh?" indicating the red garb of the stranger. "Those boys are pulling something big. Well, here's luck."

Once more the man became the center of attraction; the throngs were converging; the colors of the two universities were everywhere. A group of students followed them across the gangplank. The detective was keeping a close eye, but strangely enough the students seemed just as much mystified as himself, albeit keenly appreciative of such a liberal display of their colors. The crowd split up, some heading for the upper decks, others making a rush for the newsstands. The detective, feeling hungry, purchased a box of chocolates. He passed one to his companion.

But the other was doubtful; he shook his head.

"I am afraid I had better not try your food," he spoke. "Your air is wonderful; but I might not be able to stand the eating. After a while, when I have become acclimated—maybe yes."

"Hey?" The detective stopped in his tracks. What could the fellow mean? "Dammit," he exclaimed, "I don't get you at all. What's your name? Mine's Flanning. Sam Flanning. And for your information, I'll warn you I'm a detective. So don't pull nothing illegal. However, I sure love mystery. What's the name?"

The other straightened; his youth was magnetic; his words more so.

"Thank you, Mr. Flanning," he answered. "Glad indeed!

14

THE SPOT OF LIFE

My name is Senestro. The Bar Senestro—of the royal line of Kospia, heir to D'Hartia and Lord of the Bars."

The detective was puffing prodigiously; his mouth flopped open; then suddenly, he grasped the point. He grinned.

"Sure," he answered loftily. "I understand. Just as plain as mud. Kid, you're a good one. King of the Caspian Sea, eh? Sure enough. I might have known it. And a full blooded Red. Bolsheviki! Uhuh! I get you. Johnny on the spot."

Samuel J. Flanning wanted ground to stand on. He led the way to the prow of the boat where they could peer down at the heavy, gray heave of the water. A San Francisco mist was swirling its last minute's rush before breaking under the California sun. Like all Native Sons he was eager to boost his climate. Just now, he was standing with his legs spread, the smoke curling from his cigarette.

"Good old Frisco fog," he breathed deeply. "She'll split in a moment, and you'll see the sun."

The other stood still, a queer expectant look upon his handsome face. For some reason, every move of the crowd seemed to interest him; he turned and gazed down at the water, and then out where the sun was lightening up the fog mist.

"So you are looking for Hal Watson?" asked the detective. "Great player that; but I don't think he can come up to the mark set by his old dad when I was a boy. The old man is Professor Watson now—but at that time he was Chick Watson—All-American. But tell me, stranger—I can't get your idea. You look to me like a walking emblem for Stanford. Hal Watson is the California captain. What's the answer?"

A line of white combers was racing across the bow. The youth was watching; but at the other's questions he turned.

"Didn't I tell you that I am a Bar? We have a right to

our colors. And I have a reason for going to Dwight Way. Perhaps—"

He reached into his pocket and drew forth some gold—strange coins—the likes of which the detective had never seen—for they were not circular like ordinary money; rather, they were flat bars, shaped like small sticks of chewing gum. The officer picked one up. It was curiously coined, with the imprint of a dreamy, bubble-like city stamped across the face. But common sense wouldn't allow him to accept it at its face value; he shook his head.

"Brass?" he grunted. "What are you advertising—some picture?"

Each moment was adding to the officer's befuddlement. The shifting, scudding fog had suddenly broken, cleaving a white way for the blazing sun. The youth peered straight into its face. An exclamation of surprise—almost agony, sprang from his lips.

The detective seized him by the arm; several men crowded around. Everybody was convinced of the same thing; here was a man pulling some sort of stunt.

"What is it?" came the inevitable question. "What is it all about?"

The detective led his companion to the inside of the boat; the youth's expression was too real. No wonder Flanning could not understand.

"Search me," he answered, "I picked him up on Market Street. Says he's a Bar, whatever that is. But I can't get his stuff at all. There was no fake about the way he looked at the sun. But he looks like a good kid. I'll stay with him and watch him."

He might have added that he would be watching for a good long while; but Detective Flanning did not know. The half blinded youth was recovering; he groped with one hand.

16

THE SPOT OF LIFE

"It is wonderful," he was saying. "Your sun! Terrible, magnificent! The Jarados himself could never have described it. But I have seen. It is enough."

"Yeah," puzzled the detective, "it's the sun. But we see it every day, don't we? It's been there a million years and it will be there a million years longer. Boy, you've got me guessing. I'm ready to bite. Name your game and I'll stick with you."

We pause here to take note of a strange parallel. Understand, we had forgotten the original mystery, Otherwise this man looking at the sun would have recalled another case many years before of a man who had never seen the sun. And Samuel Flanning, fully warned, would have been able to ward off the calamity. He could have jailed this Bar Senestro. But thirty years is a long time. The heroes of bygone years become shadows; mysteries drift into myths and are forgotten. So no one can blame Detective Samuel J. Flanning.

The boat had entered the Key Route slip; the youth had recovered his composure. The two men hurried across the gangplank, boarded a Berkeley train. The Senestro sat by the window; the detective next to the aisle. Over in the east they could see the blue skies and the green hills of Contra Costa. Men were talking, women laughing; but the stranger had become sober. He kept looking across the stretch of water, gleaming blue under the sun. The detective spoke:

"Fine day, isn't it?"

"Beautiful. Your world is strange. I would like to prolong my visit. But first I must see this man Watson. After that—"

No wonder the detective kept prodding himself to get his bearings. He was sure the man was not crazy; so he went back to his original assumption of a hoax. He decided to direct the fellow to Dwight Way, and then cross over to the stadium.

17

THE SPOT OF LIFE

That would be easy.

However, it was not as easy as he thought. The youth drew attention. What with his garb, his peculiar poise, his athletic beauty, he became the focus of a crowd as they alighted in Berkeley. But the sight of the hard boiled detective explained a great deal. The American public has become accustomed to all manner of stunts. The throng hurried on. The detective and his strange companion turned into Dwight Way. Shortly afterwards they arrived at the home of Professor Chalmers Watson. The officer pointed.

"Here we are," he spoke at last. "Yonder is the house—the one behind the old fashioned iron fence."

The Bar Senestro crossed the street, opened the gate, started up the sidewalk. The detective continued on towards the stadium; but suddenly he stopped.

"Shucks!" he muttered. "He wanted to see Hal Watson. But Hal isn't there, of course. He'll see his father. Huh! I wonder."

Samuel J. Flanning was curious. He retraced his steps. Halfway down the block he could see the Senestro standing between the gate and the house. A door opened; some one —Professor Watson—came out. He was athletic, slightly over middle age. The detective worked closer, listening. The professor had stopped dead in his tracks, like a man who has seen an apparition. One hand had gone to his throat; his words wheezed.

"Senestro! The Bar Senestro! Here on earth! The Blind Spot! My God! It is open!"

Strange words!

The detective was frozen in his tracks. What was it all about? Here was more mystery! A Blind Spot! Flanning crouched behind a tree. The tall man was answering; his words were silky, insinuating, suggestive.

"Professor Watson. The immortal Chick Watson! Yes, indeed. Chick Watson, the child of the Jarados and the key to the Blind Spot! I salute thee. The Senestros are not to be denied. Yes. We have opened the Blind Spot!"

There was hesitation for a moment. Professor Watson was plainly puzzled. He gazed helplessly up and down the street. But at last he pointed towards the house, the two men ascended the steps; the door slammed.

The detective shivered. What in the world could it mean? What was the Blind Spot?

III

PROFESSOR CHALMERS WATSON

AND NOW for a few words concerning Professor Watson, better known in his youth as Chick, the father of the man who, on this day, was to lead the California varsity against the hordes of Stanford. But we are not interested in the son just at present. Let us explain.

Chalmers C. Watson was Professor of Philosophy at the University of California. A great man and one well qualified for the position—a disciple of the Spinoza school of thought, teaching the fundamental truth of a great and guiding force acting through the laws of nature—a man accustomed to summarize immortal facts in a few terse statements, and on top of that a man of tremendous mystery.

In fact, there had always been something illusive about Professor Watson. He had a past. No man could listen to him without being convinced of that one fact. His presence emanated wisdom. When you looked into his eyes, you could sense it. Here was one who had gone down into the depths, who knew all things, and did not wish to tell. We take his own words:

"There are many things which Man should not know. Woe unto him who passes knowledge on to his fellow beings, before they are strong enough to handle it."

This, indeed, was his favorite axiom. Naturally his audiences were varied; and as a matter of course, there were many of the philosophically bent, who had a leaning for the Occult. They were convinced that this great Doctor could lead them into vast fields of thought; but the professor always shook his head.

20

THE SPOT OF LIFE

"Cling with the tools you can handle; in time you will grasp the rest."

In his early life he had been an engineer; and he had never forsaken the equations of mathematics. He was one of the first to grasp the full significance of atomic structures and the planetary likeness of proton and ion; together with the forces underneath. He would snap out sudden truths:

"Man," he taught, "can conceive of space; but never of limitation. It is not until we speak of the end of space that we become baffled. We can understand neither beginning nor end; for the simple reason that these words are finite. Even a child will ask what happened before the beginning—what is on the other side of the end.

"So why speak of them?

"And with Space we must accept the theory of Universal Force. Call this ether, electricity—what you will. It remains the father of all nature—of the elements, mind, spirit. All things are possible under its multitudinous manifestation; but before we delve into the Occult, we must examine this universal power, understand it, and know. Then, perhaps, we shall be masters of our own destiny. We are pigmies now; in the end we shall be giants."

Such was Professor Watson—the man who had turned from blunt engineering into the mysterious realm of metaphysics; the man who taught his son to stand with both feet on the ground. Those of us who remember, knew him as the son-in-law and successor of Professor Holcomb—that mysterious and now legendary character who had disappeared on the eve of his lecture on the Blind Spot; but we had forgotten. All we know is that it created a great stir while it lasted.

But life is like that. The revolutions of yester-year become the myths of today. Such is fame!

Nevertheless, any one could see that there was mystery

21

locked in the past of Professor Watson. He seldom spoke of his great predecessor; and we have no record of his ever mentioning the Blind Spot.

We can wonder at this because of what followed. Perhaps the man foresaw the end—realized that some day his life would be forfeit. The years had passed. The young man who had ascended the chair of philosophy had attained a ripe middle age. His wife had passed to the great beyond; and another Watson, the one we had come to know as Hal, had risen to manhood. Today he had reached the pinnacle of collegiate athletics, heralded as an All-American and captain of his varsity. A proud father was prepared to watch his son's triumph.

But we know now that this was not to be.

Something had happened; and an obscure detective had reopened the world's greatest mystery. Next morning the papers were ringing with news of the Blind Spot!

IV

SOMEBODY BECKONS

WE RETURN now to Samuel J. Flanning, the detective with a hunch.

Flanning had watched the two men enter the house. He did not understand. The crowds had grown deeper. The detective loitered. At length the door opened. Two men stepped to the veranda; one was the professor; the other the Bar Senestro. But now the Senestro was clothed in American garb, an overcoat, and a gray slouch hat; clad thus, he looked like an ordinary citizen.

The two men were talking. Flanning sensed a strange undercurrent; the professor was excited. The other backed towards the gate. The detective caught the words:

"The Blind Spot! Two eighty-eight Chatterton Place!"

The Senestro walked down Dwight Way. The detective glanced at his watch, felt of his big game ticket. For one whole moment he was undecided; then he turned and followed. Twenty minutes later he watched his man board a Key Route train bound for San Francisco, heading for the smoker. The detective bought a paper. He had forgotten about the game; he was following something bigger.

Then came the boat; and the Ferry Building. The crowd passed over the gangplank—through a darkened exit into Market Street. The Senestro hailed a taxicab. Flanning did likewise. Next minute the old game of hide and seek was on. The Senestro was driven to Geary Street, thence up the hill and off into a maze of short cuts. The district was new to the detective. But at length the driver slowed up, called back to his fare. .

THE SPOT OF LIFE

"Here we are, sir. Your man has just gone around the corner."

Flanning alighted; sure enough, the Senestro was just ahead, walking swiftly, climbing the steps of a brownstone house. A door opened; the man disappeared. Flanning selected the steps of an apartment house on the near side of the street, sat down. Carefully he read the number of the house that he was watching—288. A wind was blowing in from the Golden Gate; it was cold and cutting; he shivered.

Understand, Detective Flanning was working on a hunch. There was always a possibility of a false scent; and yet—his intuition told him different.

Ten minutes passed. The time dragged into a half hour, during which he studied the front of the house; it was drab, dismal, lifeless, two stories high, with old fashioned yellow shutters at the windows. A feeling of gloom was in the air. The wind had stirred a fog from the Pacific. Detective Flanning shoved up his collar.

Somehow every building on the street was the same. He noticed the neighboring houses. They were cheerless wooden structures painted a drab forlorn gray. No one was in sight.

But at last a door of a neighboring building opened. A face peered forth, cautiously, for all the world as if the owner was afraid to venture into the street. Finally an old lady stepped forth; she was clutching a ragged shawl about her chin. Her hands were bony. She appeared to be intensely interested in the doings at the place with the brown front, stopping before it, wagging her head fearfully. Then she climbed the stairs of the house on the other side. Once more a door opened and another old lady stepped out. For a moment they conferred; pointing towards the other building. Then they passed inside.

Somehow their actions were foreboding. The detective

24

wondered. The women were witch-like and uncanny; their faces dried and withered. Flanning lit a cigarette.

"Shucks," he grumbled. "I have been fooled. Missed the big game and came here on a wild goose chase."

But just as he was about to depart a door opened—the very door that he had been watching. A tall man, clad in a black robe, stepped into the opening, glanced fearfully up and down the street and then over at the detective. For a moment he seemed undecided; he beckoned with his finger.

"Come!"

Samuel J. Flanning passed over. The man at the door disappeared, but his order had been imperative. He rang the bell, waited. No one answered. So he placed his hand on the knob, walked in. There was no sound.

Strange!

Flanning was undecided; the air was weird, uncanny. The room was dark, suggestive, richly furnished. The rugs were deep, somber. But there was no one in sight—merely a statuette of Rodin's "Thinker" in a corner. From the back of the building came a queer resonance like something bouncing along a vast corridor. The detective listened.

"Hello," he said. "Hello!"

But there was no answer—merely that ripple of vast distance. He could hear tiny bells, illusive, almost ethereal.

"Hello! Hello!" he called. "Funny! That man called me over. Why?"

Still no answer. He parted the draperies, peered within. At first he was only conscious of a red glow—and a library. But there was no occupant. The detective waited; finally he stepped over to the desk, glanced at the papers upon the surface. One was signed by a queer name—Rhamda Avec.

What the papers were, Detective Flanning could not tell. But he was sure there was something wrong. He listened! A lump rose in his throat. What was it? Two minutes before

25

he had been in the street; but already he could sense a vast lapse of time.

There it was again—a rhythm of mellifluous music, far away, tintinnabulating, floating from the distance of a faraway gallery. Flanning parted the red drapes that shut off a rear apartment; he noticed a door with a brass knob. Perhaps the sound came from there.

Something was falling. The music ceased; a struggle was going on; he heard a banging and scuffling of feet. Perhaps it was murder! Flanning threw open the door, stepped inside. And that was about his last conscious action. The rest was a blur.

First of all he was struck by some terrrific force, thrown against the side-wall, where, dazed but conscious, he watched a scene above his comprehension.

There was a light in the center of the room—a thing unholy, a coruscating iridescence, blending from blue into green and purple, blazing from the ceiling like a shimmer of frozen lightning. Flanning had never beheld anything like it, for the light was alive, racing its snake-like tendrils into the corners of the room.

And there was something else—a visibility into a vast perspective, voidlike and remote, a picture of chaos. And it was all in that one spot. Immense and weird—unearthly. But most important of all, there was a man—a man suspended above the abyss of the earth, yet beyond it.

And what a man!

The detective clutched the side-wall, his fingers spread out, his breath coming in short gasps. A man suspended in light, and that man was—the Bar Senestro.

Suspended, or at least, so it seemed!

Then—there was something else—a vast stretch and a vision of snow whiteness, with two men rushing towards the mysterious Bar. Something happened. The chaos disappeared; and the tintinnabulating bells runed an ethereal music into the detective's ears. Simultaneously, the Bar Senestro had stepped from the coruscating iridescence, rushed at the detective. He shouted:

"You have followed! Fool that you are! You would solve the secret—the Spot of Life! Come!"

By that time, Detective Flanning had recovered his senses; his nerves snapped into action; he sprang away.

That one leap saved him. The Bar made a mighty effort, lunging, but at that very second, the living flame pulsed out, caught him again within its snakelike grasp, sucked him in. The thing was instantaneous—complete. The light disappeared like a snuffed candle; the room was still.

But only for a second. The detective was stunned; everything had been ghost-like. And then! A bell!

This time a great bell—cathedral-like in its immensity—beautiful, filling the air with its music, silvery, voluminous. A church bell! One tremendous stroke! That was all. Music of the angels—dissolving slowly into nothing! The detective could stand no more; his mind went blank under the flood of magnetism. He fell flat upon his face.

V

THE BLIND SPOT

How LONG he lay there, Flanning did not know; but at last he opened his eyes, glanced about. His mind blurred. The details were shuffled and kaleidoscopic, yet vividly distinct.

Then he remembered. He had been standing on the opposite side of the street when a gentleman in a black suit had beckoned him over to the house. Yes, that was it! There was a gentleman—but he had disappeared. No one was in the place—not a soul. And there were strange sounds—and rooms of books and mystery!

Then it all came back. He recalled the last apartment and the streak of living fire, the Bar Senestro, and his own leap for safety. His mind settled on that one fact. But beyond that he could not go; something had knocked him unconscious.

He was weak and could scarcely rise.

Slowly he turned and looked about the room, his mind half working, his eyes blurred. What—what was that form on the floor beside him? The thing lay stretched out like the figure of a cross—a black shape, strangely familiar. Oh, yes—it was the body of a man. Some one dressed in a black suit—the same person who had beckoned him across the street. Perhaps—undoubtedly he was dead. Samuel J. Flanning was still in a daze. The floor was littered with papers—of the typewriter variety, scattered in wild confusion. But there was no furniture in the apartment except the rug.

The detective sat up, rubbed his eyes, reached for his revolver. Why hadn't he settled it in his own fashion? Here was murder or something very close to it. Slowly he lifted himself against the wall and dusted himself off; then he stooped over to the body, lifted it, felt of the heart. The man was not dead. He could sense the tremor of life and returning consciousness. Who could he be?

In all his life, Flanning, the detective, had never seen such a face; it was serene, as beautiful as that of a god, and old! The detective was thrilled by the contact; he heard the words:

"It—it is the Blind Spot! Beware of the Bar Senestro! Notify Professor Watson. Water! Give me water, please! Oh, for one more moment. Hurry!"

Flanning looked up. In the rear was a door. He passed through, found a kitchen, fumbled for some glasses. His hand shook as he turned on the faucet. It seemed an age. He fairly stumbled. Then—there it was again!

The light!—blazing that coruscating glow of unholy blue! A sense of vacuity and a sound of tremendous distance—punctuated by weird bells and tinkling footsteps. Words, shouts, commands, drifting from distant corridors! A multitude of voices, followed by one reverberation, bell-like, and silvery! The man in the other room called out:

"Hurry! Hurry! In the name of Heaven! Please hurry! It is the Blind Spot!"

Flanning crashed through the door. The water splashed from his hand. His right hand groped for his automatic. But he saw nothing to shoot at—merely the old man on the floor rising and falling in a spasmodic effort to reach the safety of the wall, his features terrified, frozen. Flanning was never to forget it—the doomed creature was jerking himself along, and that racing unholy light was dancing after him. The coruscation appeared to widen, pulsing like a living thing, acting like a magnet; objects were lifting, whirling into an unseen vortex. Then—

It was the bell! One peal! The light snuffed out. The detective fired instinctively—but the report did not shut out the sound. Some one laughed, a mocking, humming taunt of derision. The room roared, returned to normal.

The body of the old man had disappeared!

Detective Flanning did not stir; he was frozen to the floor. Here was mystery beyond belief. It was impossible—yet it had happened.

But he was still the detective. It was his business to arrive at solutions. He thought of the police.

The police? Immediately he retracted the idea. Subconsciously he pictured himself relating his story and being laughed at. That would never do. But—and his thoughts redoubled—what was this Blind Spot? He recalled the exclamation of Professor Watson.

"The Blind Spot is open!"

Detective Flanning was a man of hard nerves; he was shaken, but he would not be baffled. He stepped into the room, taking care to avoid the center. It was empty except for a rug upon the floor. Flanning lifted this up. Nothing there! Then he examined the sides; there were two doors, one on either end—nothing else—not even a spot upon the wall. He thought of a secret apartment and turned back; but just then he noticed a crumpled paper in a far corner; he walked over and picked it up. It was typewritten, single-spaced, but plainly many years old. The white paper had become yellow; it almost cracked in his hands as he read it:

She opened the door. Jerome entered and took off his hat; judicially he repeated the doctor's name to keep in her mind. She closed the door carefully and touched his arm. It seemed to him that she was terribly weak and tottering; her old eyes, however expressionless, were full of pitiful pleading. She was scarcely more than a shadow.

THE SPOT OF LIFE

"You are his son?"

Jerome lied; but he did it for a reason.

"Yes."

"Then come."

She took him by the sleeve and led him to a room, then across it to a door in a side-wall. Her step was slow and tottering; twice she stopped to sing the dirge of her wonder. "First a man and then a woman. Now there is one; now there are two. Now there is one. You are his son." And twice she stopped to listen: "Do you hear anything? A bell? It always makes you think of church and things that are holy. This is a beautiful bell. First—"

Either the woman was without her reason or nearly so; she was very weak and tottering.

"Come mother, I know, first a bell; but Doctor Holcomb?"

The name brought her back again. For a moment she was blank, trying to recall her senses. And then she remembered. She pointed to the door.

"In there," she spoke. "Doctor Holcomb. The little old man with the beautiful whiskers. This morning it was a man; now it is a woman. Now there are two; now there are two. Oh dear, perhaps you shall hear the bell."

Jerome began to scent a tragedy. Certainly the old lady was uncanny; the house was bare and hollow; the scant furniture was theadbare with age and mildew; each sound was exaggerated and fearful; even their breathing. He placed his hand on the knob and opened the door.

"Now there are two. Now there are two."

The room was empty. Not a bit of furniture; a blank bare apartment with an old fashioned ceiling. Nothing else. Whatever the weirdness and adventure, Jerome

31

was getting nowhere. The old lady was still clinging to his arm and still droning.

"Now there are two. Now there are two. This morning a man; now a woman. Now there are two."

"Come mother, come. This will not do. Perhaps—"

But just then the old lady's fingers clinched into his arm; her eyes grew bright; her mouth opened; and she stopped in the middle of her drone. Jerome grew rigid. And no wonder. From the middle of the room not ten feet away came the tone of a silver bell, a great voluminous sound—and music. Then as suddenly it died out and runed into nothing. At the same time he felt the fingers on his arm relax; and a heap at his feet. He reached over. The life and intelligence that was so near the line was just crossing over the border. The poor old lady! Here was a tragedy he could not understand.

He stopped to assist her. He was trembling. And as he did so, he heard the drone of her soul as it wafted to the shadow:

"Now there are two."

Samuel J. Flanning was nonplused; in all his life he had never encountered such a situation. He read the paper a second time, folded it carefully, and then reopened it and read it again. Finally he found an envelope and sealed it. His mind whirled back to the eternal question.

What was the Blind Spot?

And what was this paper? Undoubtedly, it was one of the many that had been swept into the light. And who was the man Jerome? And who was the mysterious Holcomb? And the old lady? It was all so weird, so suggestive. The room throbbed mystery; the words seemed to leap from the paper; he too, could hear the dirge of the old lady's warning:

"Now there are two!"

THE SPOT OF LIFE

But this would never do; Samuel J. Flanning shook off the feeling. First of all, he would go over the house and learn what it was all about. In a few moments he had completed the tour of the lower apartments, of which there were six, three of them lined with books, a sort of reception room, a bedroom and a kitchen; then he ascended the creaking stair to the second story.

Here he found five rooms, dusty, dirty, three of them empty; the two others evidently used for storerooms were littered with odds and ends. Speaking in terms of a dwelling the place was capacious; but there was no sign of human occupants. Slowly he returned to the lower floor.

Something warned him that he had looked at a murder; that his life was in imminent danger. The feeling grew. It was good to open the front door and gaze out into the street. The fog had disappeared. Sunset was painting the western sky. He could see the blue waters of San Francisco Bay. And how good it looked! He stepped outside, peered up and down the street. Everything was real; just as it should be. Newsboys were calling.

"Paper, paper! Extra! Big mystery!"

He stumbled down the steps, walked to the corner and bumped into an urchin who was yelling with all the force of his lungs.

"Extra! Extra! Professor Watson found dead! Professor Watson! Dead! Father of Hal Watson—Captain of the California varsity. Dead!"

In two leaps Detective Samuel J. Flanning was upon the boy, shoving a coin into his hand. His eyes caught the glaring headlines:

"Professor Chalmers Watson stricken by death! Famous philosopher and old-time athlete dies at the moment of his son's triumph! Found on library floor!"

VI

CHECKING UP

HERE WAS murder sure enough. Detective Flanning was convinced. He called in the police. His story created a sensation. A checkup followed. The newspapers pounced upon the story, doubted, and made the best of it by asking questions. The headlines ran:

"What is the Blind Spot?"

"Professor Watson's death revives old mystery."

"Murder hinted!"

Then they went into details. But people can only believe so much; and besides, the reporters, scenting a hoax, had cleverly given it a skeptical angle. What's more, the post mortem proved beyond a doubt that Professor Chalmers Watson had died a natural death—plain prosaic heart failure. The hint of murder was exploded into a cocked hat. That let out the police.

The detective was up against it. However, the affair had revived the dim legend of the Blind Spot. The story became a sensation for several days; and lacking other news, the papers played it up and asked the question:

"What is the Blind Spot?"

What connection, if any, had the professor of philosophy at the University of California with the mystery? And why had the mysterious man in black asked the detective to summon Doctor Watson? Was it all a hoax? And most important of all, who was the illusive Bar Senestro? Hundreds had seen him that day on Market Street; but most of them had accepted him as a student out on a prank. No one dreamed of the Occult—Samuel Flanning least of all.

34

THE SPOT OF LIFE

The detective hunted up the son of the dead professor.

Hal Watson proved to be everything that could be asked of young American manhood, tall, broad shouldered, red-haired, with cold gray eyes and firm features, a youth born to lead, and yet though the boy was bowed with sorrow, he was eager to render assistance.

The detective related his story—glad to discover an appreciative audience. It was a beautiful California day. The sun was shining with a tantalizing warmth. A child was playing upon the lawn.

"I don't know so much about father's past," spoke the youth in answer to the question, "but there must have been something. There was always a lapse of years that he did not mention. He would talk freely about his boyhood and about his days in college; but after that, there was a period of years which he chose to regard a blank. I don't know why."

"I see," answered Flanning. "Lots of people are like that. Did he ever mention the Blind Spot?"

"Not that I recall, but there were times when he was strangely moody; when he would sit, day after day, just thinking."

"And this Professor Holcomb was your grandfather, was he not?"

"Yes. My mother's father. My mother, you know, passed away shortly after I was born. That was about the time my father assumed the chair of philosophy."

The detective nodded.

"How about Professor Holcomb? Did you ever hear of his being connected with the Blind Spot?"

Hal Watson frowned.

"It's hard for me to remember," he said. "You see, I have never given it much thought. This thing was kept from me, purposely, I suppose; but come to think of it, my grand-

THE SPOT OF LIFE

father did disappear rather suddenly. He was an Occultist, you know, and he entertained his own theory regarding metaphysics—not a spiritualist, you understand; but something deeper. His disappearance, I believe, happened on the eve of a famous lecture on the Occult; and—come to think of it now—I have heard it somewhere—that lecture had to do with some sort of spot. Perhaps it was this Blind Spot you speak of."

"And this Senestro?" asked the detective. "You didn't see. him, of course. But was there some one else in the house who did?"

The youth nodded.

"Wait a minute," he said.

He stepped to the door, disappeared. A few moments later he returned with a little old lady clad in black silk; she was dabbing her eyes with a lace handkerchief.

"This is Miss Stearns, our housekeeper," he announced. "She will tell you what she knows."

The spinster sat down, looking from Hal Watson to the detective. Plainly she was excited. But the detective gained her confidence in almost a moment.

"Yes, sir. Yes, sir," she answered in response to the detective's question. "There was some one here that afternoon. Professor Watson was just getting ready to go up to the stadium. I remember because he spoke to me only a few moments before.

"He was saying something to me about the prospects of winning and hoping that our team would get the breaks. Then he said good-by and started for the door.

"He must have returned, for a moment later I heard him talking to some one in the library. His voice was strange; but not as much so as that of the other. I could not make out what they were saying. It was none of my affair, you understand. Yet I was interested in that new voice; it held such a wonderful tone, so sweet and forceful, and insistent. Whoever he was, the man seemed assured of what he was saying. The professor's voice, on the other hand, was full of alarm. He kept saying: 'No, no, no!' And he was begging for I know not what."

"You didn't distinguish the words, so how do you know this?"

"By the intonation. One doesn't have to hear each syllable to understand that men are in an argument. Of course, I really had no business listening at all."

"And I, on the other hand, wish that you had listened a great deal more," answered the detective. "It might have saved a world of trouble. Did you see the professor?"

"Not for several minutes," came the reply. "They would talk for a while, and then lapse into silence. I only remember two words. The professor called him 'Bar Senestro.' He addressed him that way several times. He kept denying the thing the other requested. Finally he walked to the door and ascended the stairs. When he came down, he was carrying some clothes—an overcoat, a hat, and a suit. I think he had some shoes. I did not get a glimpse of his guest. There was silence after that and I returned to the rear of the house. The two men must have walked out on the front porch. They went as far as the gate, perhaps. Anyway, a while later, the professor returned alone and entered the library."

"You did not see this stranger at all?"

"No sir, I was a trifle ashamed of what I had done. But, then, I just happened to be in the next room."

"What happened after the professor returned to the library?"

"Nothing. There was no sound so I concluded he had gone up to the stadium. I was at the back of the building; but after a while I had occasion to walk to the front door.

THE SPOT OF LIFE

I glanced into the library. The professor was seated at his desk, sprawled out in a chair. Even then I didn't know what happened. I walked in, and—and—Professor Watson was dead!"

The detective nodded; the old lady dabbed her eyes with her handkerchief; the youth listened intently.

"How long have you been with Professor Watson and his family?" asked the detective.

"For about twenty years," came the answer. "I came here shortly after the death of Hal's mother. I knew her as a girl."

"Ah." The detective straightened up. "Then perhaps you remember her father, Professor Holcomb?"

"Yes, I do. That is, in a way," came the reply. "He was a great man. And—and he—he died of this Blind Spot just like Doctor Watson."

Here was news indeed. The two men drew up their chairs. The old lady trembled. The detective spoke:

"You say the first professor, the great Doctor Holcomb, died of the Blind Spot? How do you know this? Did you ever hear any one say it; or did Professor Watson—"

She shook her head.

"No, sir, Professor Watson was always reticent about such matters; it just happened by chance. It must have been about ten years ago. I was rummaging up in the attic when I picked up a crumpled piece of paper. It was part of a manuscript; I read it and have always remembered."

"Have you this paper?"

The old lady stood up. "I'll get it."

She disappeared through the door, leaving the two men alone. The detective nodded.

"Now we're getting somewhere," he said. "Looks like we're on the track of an almighty big thing. Whatever the Blind Spot is, it reached out for your father and your

38

grandfather. Both of them dead! Nice prospect, eh? Boy, I'm thinking you and I will have to form a company."

"I'll say," came the dubious answer. "Looks like I've got a job. My father and my grandfather! Straight down the line!"

The old lady returned; she began pulling some paper from an envelope; the sheets were crumpled and torn, yellow with age, but still legible. The detective's fingers shook as he held them to the light. Hal Watson looked over his shoulder. They read:

Man, let me tell you, is egotistic. All our philosophies are based on ego. We live three score years and we balance it with all Eternity. We are IT. Did you ever stop and think of Eternity? It is a rather long time. What right have we to say that Life, which we assume to be everlasting, immediately becomes retrospect once it passes out of the conscious individuality which it was allotted on this earth? The trouble is ourselves. We are five-sensed. We weigh everything with our senses. Every thing. We so measure Eternity. Until we step into other senses, which undoubtedly exist, we shall never arrive at the conception of Infinity. Now I am going to make a startling announcement.

The past five years have promised a culmination which has been guessed at and yearned for since the beginning of time. It is within, and still without, the scope of metaphysics. Those of you who have attended my lectures have heard me call myself the material idealist. I am a mystic sensationalist. I believe that we can derive nothing from pure contemplation. There is mystery and wonder in the veil of the Occult. The Earth, our Life, is merely the vestibule of the Universe. Contemplation alone will hold us all as inept and as impotent as the old monks of Athos. We have a mountan of literature behind us, all contemplative, and whatever its wisdom, it has given us not one thing outside of the abstract. From Plato down to the present, our philosophy has given us not one tangible proof, not one concrete fact that we can put our hands on. We are virtually where we were originally; and we can talk, talk, talk from now until the clap of Doomsday.

What then?

My friends, philosophy must take a step sidewise. In this modern age young science, practical science, has grown up and far surpassed us. We must go back to the beginning, forget our subjective musings and enter the concrete. We are five-sensed, and in the nature of the case, we must bring the proof down into the concrete where we can understand it. Can we pierce the nebulous screen that shuts us out of the Occult? We have reached for the curtain many times and found it missing. We have doubted, laughed at ourselves, and been laughed at; but the fact remains that we have always persisted in believing.

I have said that we shall never, never understand Infinity while within the limitations of our five senses. I repeat it. But that does not infer that we shall never solve some of the mystery of Life. The Occult is not only a supposition but a fact. We have peopled it with terror because, like our forebears before Columbus, we have peopled it with imagination.

And now to my statement.

I have called myself the Material Idealist. I have adopted an entirely new trend of philosophy. During the past few years, unknown to you and unknown to my friends, I have allied myself with practical science. I desire something concrete; while my colleagues and others were pounding out tomes upon tomes of powerful sophistry, I have been pounding away at the screen of the Occult.

This is a proud moment.

I have succeeded. Tomorrow I shall bring you the fact and the substance. I have lifted up the curtain and flooded it with the light of day. You shall have the fact for your senses. Tomorrow I shall explain it all. I shall deliver my greatest lecture, in which my whole life has come to a focus. It is not spiritualism nor sophistry. It is concrete fact and common sense. The subject of my lecture will be "THE BLIND SPOT."

Here begins the second part.

We know now that the great lecture was never delivered. Immediately the news was scattered upon the campus. It became common property. It was spread over the country and was featured in all the great metropolitan dailies. In the lecture room, next morning, seats were at a premium; students, professors, instructors, and all the prominent people who could gain admission crowded into the hall; even the irrepressible reporters had stolen in to take down this greatest scoop of the century. The place was jammed until even standing room was unthought of. The crowd, dense and packed, and physically uncomfortable, waited.

Ten minutes dragged by. It was a long, long wait. But at last the bell rang that ticked the hour. Everyone was expectant. And then fifteen minutes passed by, twenty. At length one of the colleagues stepped into the doctor's office and telephoned his home. His daughter answered.

"Papa? Why he left two hours ago for the campus."

"About what time?"

"It was about seven thirty. You know he is to deliver his lecture today on the Blind Spot. I wanted to hear

41

it but he told me I could have it at home. He said he was to have a wonderful guest and I must make ready to receive him. Isn't papa there?"

"Not yet. Who is this wonderful guest? Did he say?"

"Oh, yes, in a way. A most wonderful man. And he gave him a strange name—Rhamda Avec. I remember because it was so funny. I asked papa if he were Sanskrit; and he said that he is much older than that. Just imagine!"

"Did your father have his lecture with him?"

"Oh yes. He glanced over it at breakfast. He told me he was going to startle the world as it had never been since the days of Columbus."

"Indeed!"

"Yes, and he was terribly impatient. He said he had to be at the college at eight to receive the great man. He was to deliver his lecture at ten. And afterward we would have lunch and he would give me the whole story. I am all impatience."

"Thank you."

Then he went back and made the announcement that there was a little delay but that Doctor Holcomb would be there shortly. But he was not. At twelve o'clock there were still some people waiting. At one o'clock the last man had slipped from the room and wondered. In all the country there was but one man who knew. That one was an obscure man who had yielded to a detective's intuition and fallen inadvertently upon one of the greatest mysteries of modern times.

The detective whistled, passed the paper over to his companion. The youth read it a second time. At last he looked up. The other nodded.

"Now we have it," he said. "Things are beginning to dovetail. The detective mentioned here was undoubtedly the selfsame Jerome who figures in the paper I found over at 288 Chatterton Place. Can't you see, Hal? It was your grandfather who first learned the secret of this uncanny Blind Spot. He merely tackled something too big for him. He disappeared, and your father must have followed behind him. That would account for those five missing years. Perhaps he learned too much. But he could not avoid the penalty. It got him in the end. And who is this Detective Jerome?"

Samuel J. Flanning turned to the old lady; he spoke kindly.

"Tell me," he asked, "why didn't you show this paper before? For instance, to the police?"

"Because I was afraid," came the answer. "Besides, I felt that they would laugh at me."

VII

JIMMY FUILLARD

THERE WAS no backing out now. Hal Watson was gazing into the street. He turned the paper in his hand, compared it with the one the detective had found at 288 Chatterton Place.

The texture was the same. Both men noted that at once.

"If we can find more," said Hal Watson, "we shall have something to go on. I will ransack this house thoroughly. And we must do the same over there—learn all we can about father and my old granddad. They were great men, both of them."

"Then you are with me," said the detective, stepping forward. "Thanks!"

The old lady suddenly came to life again. She spoke up:

"There was just one more thing, Mr. Flanning. It was a long time ago. Perhaps it has nothing to do with this Blind Spot but I have always remembered it."

"What was it?"

"There was an old man," she said. "He came here about fifteen years ago, and held a long conversation with Professor Watson. I recall him distinctly because of his appearance. He seemed to be Oriental but at the same time Caucasian. As straight as an arrow and tall—dark hair and wonderful eyes. A man who was plainly old and yet wonderfully youthful. The professor held him in tremendous regard; he had a remarkable name—Rhamda Avec."

"Ah!" the detective nodded. "That is the name I found on the paper—Rhamda Avec. Anything more?"

"No, that is all. I don't know why, but I always associated him with the Blind Spot."

Miss Stearns was dismissed. The two men were left alone. Hal Watson had become silent; suddenly he straightened.

He reached for the phone, asked for San Francisco, gave a number. He held his hand over the mouthpiece as he waited. Then:

"I'm asking for one Jimmy Fuillard," he spoke. "I'll tell you in a minute." Then—as the answer came over the wire: "He's not there? Oh, I see. Out of town. Up in the northern part of the State? Won't be back for several days? Thank you."

He hung up, turned to the expectant detective.

"I just happened to remember," he explained. "Jimmy Fuillard is an old friend—an attorney over in San Francisco. He asked me something about the Blind Spot about a month ago. It was at a social function. And we didn't have much opportunity to talk. But I remember now. Said he wanted to speak to me when he had a chance. There was a little German with him whom he introduced as a second Einstein—a man named Van Tassel. Of course I didn't know what he was talking about. Didn't pay any attention."

They journeyed over to San Francisco, drove up to headquarters. Detective Flanning introduced his companion to Chief O'Bannion.

The big man listened, nodded.

"All right," he said, "it's up to you, Flanning. Dig into it for all you're worth. But" with a smile—"don't come back with any more ghost stories. Find the facts. If anything turns up, report it at once. We'll be waiting."

Next they visited the Hall of Records, looked up the title to the property at 288 Chatterton. The house was owned under two names, those of Rhamda Avec and Chalmers C. Watson. Furthermore, they learned that the property had formerly belonged to one Harry Wendell and had been sold for delinquent taxes. The detective scratched his head.

"There's another detail. Why did this Harry Wendell default in his taxes? Do you think—"

"The Blind Spot," answered Hal Watson. "Everything drifts to calamity. I must take a look."

An hour later they turned into Chatterton Place, stopped across the street from the building. Once again a fog was shivering up from the ocean; the same dingy gloom was in the air. Hal Watson glanced at the other.

"Do you get it?" the officer asked. "The thing clutches at your throat. Let's cross over."

At that instant the door of a neighboring house opened; an old lady tottered down the steps, clutching a brown shawl about her head. She gazed at the two men. The detective spoke:

"Pardon me. Can you tell me who lives in this house?"

She clutched the shawl tighter, a frightened look in her eyes.

"Who are you?" Her words were scarcely audible.

"A detective."

"Oh!" she shivered. "Then the police have finally woke up. It's about time. But it will do you no good. The old gentleman—"

She stopped, looking from one to another. Her thin lips framed the words:

"Did—did Jimmy Fuillard send you?"

"No. I'm a friend—"

"If he didn't send you I'd rather not say a word. I don't know anything about it. It's all mysterious and uncanny. I can't say. Jimmy told me not to talk." She turned back up the steps, looking back fearfully at the two men. "Don't ask me. And don't go into that house. You'll be sorry."

The door slammed. Hal Watson felt a quiver run through his marrow; he nodded grimly,

"Don't know as I blame her. Looks like we'll have to wait for Jimmy. But let's go into the house, anyway."

46

VIII

THE HOUSE OF MYSTERY

THEY CLIMBED the steps, entered the building. The detective switched on the lights. His face was pale. "Notice anything?" he asked.

Hal did not answer. The air was still as death.

"Let's see the rest of the house," he finally said. "I never was in a place like this before. What can it be?"

The detective closed the door. In the corner of the hall was the statuette of Rodin's "Thinker," lonely and suggestive. The youth glanced and wondered; passed to the next room. The detective motioned to the walls, lined with books. A library table was in the center. Several books were spread out; one of them face down.

Hal Watson walked over, picked one up, read the title. The text was in German script—"The Critique of Pure Reason," by Kant. Near by was a Latin work, "De Intellectus Emendatione," by Spinoza. The third was another German work by Herder—"Einige Gesprachs uber Spinoza's System." The last volume was an English translation of Le Bon's "Evolution of Force." Blank papers and pencils were scattered about.

The detective spoke:

"This Rhamda Avec was a wise old bird. I didn't know there were so many books in the world. Notice the different languages. Everything here but Chinese. High power stuff. Some of those words would cramp a snake."

The younger man was impressed. Here was proof of some great spirit. This same man had been his father's partner. He turned the leaves of one of the books, thinking.

THE SPOT OF LIFE

"We don't read that stuff nowadays," he muttered. "We only admire it. Are you sure that this Rhamda Avec was the owner of this library—that he was the man who disappeared?"

"I'd swear."

Hal Watson stepped over to the wall, read the titles—metaphysical, psychological, occult, with a liberal sprinkling of the scientific. He followed the officer into the next room. It was like the first, with a door at the side.

Flanning placed his hand on the knob, held up a finger.

"Here," he announced solemnly, "is the place. Now be careful."

The apartment was empty, except for a deep Persian rug in the center. But for all that, there was a feeling of distance, isolation—chaos.

The youth drew a deep breath, listened.

"What is it?" he asked at length.

But the other did not answer. Hal Watson stepped into the room. Samuel J. Flanning caught him by the sleeve. His voice came in a pleading gasp.

"Don't go," he warned. "Don't! At least, not until we find out what it is."

But Watson had slipped along the side wall, waiting. Here was a deathlike chaos—the silence of vacuum!

What could it be?

He listened. Listened. And then he heard.

There came a sound—a beautiful mellow note like a bird singing in a vast pantheon, silvery, melodious, echoing; followed by silence. For a moment! And then again the unseen warbler began—like a canary winging in full-throated flight up to the sky. Then—again silence.

Hal Watson had heard enough.

Samuel J. Flanning withdrew from the room, shut the door. He sat down, mopped his face with a handkerchief.

"Well?" he asked.

"Did the police see this?"

"No. The darn thing didn't act up when I wanted it to. I felt like a fool. The chief laughed at me. What do you think?"

"What do I think? What can I? There's something, of course. Looks like trickery."

"You don't believe in the stuff, eh? Well, neither do I. Nevertheless, facts are facts. There was your father. Why did he die?"

"You say you found that man in there?"

The detective nodded; he was a headquarters' man all over. Yet he had seen.

"In there," he pointed. "And there was that streak of blue light. And a bell! It was the most beautiful and the most tempting sound I ever heard. I was knocked out; when I regained consciousness, I was stretched on the floor. This man I call the Rhamda was spread out in the middle of the room."

"What did he look like?"

"Tall, dark, dressed in black—looked like a high priest. Remarkable face. He was dying. I could see that. Asked for water and spoke about this Blind Spot. You know the rest. I was in the kitchen when he called again. Then there was this blue light. I tore into the room, but I was too late."

"It gets me," the younger man said. "I didn't suppose it could approximate so much mystery."

The detective grunted; he nudged his thumb towards the door.

"Your grandfather went in there! And he never came out, because no one ever heard of him afterwards. And there was your own father. Where did he go? Why was he so persistently silent regarding that particular period of his life? Why did your father and this Rhamda Avec purchase this house?"

THE SPOT OF LIFE

Hal Watson did not answer. The detective stood up, tiptoed to the door, looked through. There was no sound. Finally he closed it, sat down. He lit a cigar, puffed savagely.

"The Blind Spot," he grunted. "I had never heard of such a thing. Now, all the world is covered with spots. The Occult? There's no such animal."

"Ditto," came the answer. "But still—how do we know? Let's go over the building first."

There were only two more apartments on the lower floor so they climbed the stairs, opening the rooms and gazing at the piles of odds and ends, boxes of books and old magazines, and the eternal dust that always clings to cobwebby apartments. The paper on the walls was faded; the floor was moldy. Empty bottles lay here and there, together with some dilapidated furniture. The air was dank and close.

Finally the detective stopped at a door near the rear of the building, where a narrow, corkscrew stair led them into a small apartment.

"I want you to take a look at this laboratory," he said. "Understand, I haven't touched a thing. Every article is where I found it."

Hal Watson stepped inside; the place was nothing unusual. Shelves containing equipment lined the walls; in one corner was a small lathe with several bars of brown soap on a table; close by was a small motor. However, there was something else—in the middle of the room, resting on a heavy, asbestos covered work bench were several instruments, of complicated and unusual design. At first glance they resembled a set of intricate microscopes fitted with a set of binoculars near the top.

Hal was interested; he stepped closer. But just at that moment something happened. The detective had turned a switch to light the apartment. Apparently he touched the wrong one.

The motor had started!

Simultaneously, a sputtering noise issued from the instrument—accompanied by a peculiar whistling *brrrr*. Streaks of bluish light leaped from the two poles, meeting halfway and forming a peculiar bubble of incandescence.

Hal Watson was fascinated.

The white dot was something he had never seen—for all the world like an atomic sun. It was growing larger, spinning itself into substance. The youth leaned over, his eyes intent, hands trembling. He glanced at the detective.

"What's the matter?"

Hal pointed: "Can't you see?" he said. "It—Lord, Flanning, don't you grasp it? Watch that dot. Substance out of nothing. The secret of the atom—the building up of matter! Don't touch a thing in this room. Leave everything as it is. We must learn the secret."

But the detective's reaction was entirely different. The bluish flame and that core of incandescence reminded him too much of the Blind Spot. He caught his companion by the arm. He was just in time.

Bang!

The room was filled with bluish flame; the men reeled against the side wall, blinded, almost unconscious. Then—everything was silent. Hal Watson pulled himself together, rushed to his companion.

"Are you hurt?"

The officer opened his eyes, staggered to his feet. "I guess I'm O.K. How about yourself? Wait a minute, I'll shut off the power. What happened?"

Several bottles had been broken; the room was full of acrid smoke. The set of instruments had been destroyed. Nothing remained except a mass of fused metal—not a single piece left for identification. Hal Watson picked up a rod from the table and began spreading the bits of hot metal. Suddenly he found what he wanted—an object as large as a canary's egg, white as new-fallen snow.

"There it is," he muttered. "Whatever happened to the instruments, we still have the product. Wonder what it is?"

It was a curious moment. Hal Watson stepped closer, touched the object with the rod, pulled it to one side. The heat from the fused metal was intense.

"Don't touch it," exclaimed the detective.

Hal Watson had no such intention; instead, he reached for the water faucet, filled a glass tumbler, poured the contents upon the stone. Perhaps he expected a sizzle of steam; but there was a far different reaction. The water curdled into a milky white, coating itself about the jewel.

Ice!

Instantaneous, almost impossible! Out of heat had come frigidity! Both men leaned forward. Hal Watson was about to touch it, when the other cautioned him again.

"Don't do it! If it's that cold, it would stick to your flesh. Here!"

He passed him a rag. Watson carried it to the light.

"A miracle!" he exclaimed. "We saw it with our own eyes. This Rhamda Avec was no ordinary mortal. This law is atomic; nothing else."

"What do you mean?"

"Simply this. You have been looking at a piece of exalted alchemy—the building up of substance out of energy. Our friend Rhamda possessed the law—the secret of the atom, its composition and control. You, yourself, turned on the power."

"Electricity!"

"Call it what you will. It is the fundamental energy from which all matter is composed—silver, helium, sulphur, gold—a mere matter of ions and protons, their collocation and control. If you possess that law you can build up the universe."

"Then this is an element?"

"At least it is a fact," came the answer. "Wonder what this stuff is?"

Once again he picked it up. It was not diamond; although there was a suggestion of similarity, There were no sharp edges; the surface was as smooth as a pigeon's egg, snow-white, its weight about that of ordinary bull-quartz. With a deft movement he dropped it into a tumbler of water, watched an additional miracle. The liquid was solidified into transparent ice. Puzzled at the sudden change, Hal turned the glass upside down, tapped the bottom with an iron rod and watched the contents slip out—a solid lump with the stone in the frozen core!

"I'll be—" from the detective.

Hal Watson nodded.

"Undoubtedly," he answered, "something to do with your Blind Spot. I'd give my right leg if I could get in touch with this Rhamda Avec. But listen!"

Hal Watson had grown rigid; his arm lifted.

A peculiar sound was coming from the lower floor; the atmosphere had suddenly become magnetic—pregnant with intensity, suspense.

"What was it?" from the detective.

Then—the magnetism was gone; the undercurrent of sound broke into a melodious tinkling of tiny bells, drifting into the faraway distance—like the suggestion of illusion. And then again—

This time there was a muffled roar—the voice of a multitude, clamorous, indistinct, tumultuous! Both men leaped for the stairway, rushed to the room of the Blind Spot.

There it was!

THE SPOT OF LIFE

The string of incandescence was whirling around the core of blue; shimmering, spreading into a transparent reality; finally fading out upon a round white surface, shaped like a gigantic dais! Then—they beheld the depth of an unknown distance, surmounted by water spouts reaching to the heavens, shot through with the roar of voices and the color of storm, titanic, immeasurable!

What was it?

The panorama was instantaneous; then, something blurred. In its place was that string of bluish light, dropping from the ceiling. That, and a mighty sound!

A bell! Great, sonorous, like all the tones of the earth woven into one! Musical! Just one stroke! And that was all!

IX

BEHIND THE PANEL

THE DETECTIVE came to first. For the second time within a week he had been overcome by the Blind Spot. The place was full of magnetism; he gathered himself together, rubbed his eyes.

Hal Watson was slumped against the wall, staring like a man in a nightmare; but suddenly he lifted one arm, came out of it.

"Well," he faltered, "what was it? Where are we? Did you see it, Flanning? So that's the Blind Spot."

The detective mopped his brow for the twelfth time; sat down. Hal Watson went on: "Let's see, Flanning. I want to get this thing straight down to the last detail. There was a dais—a snow-white substance, and a sort of stairway. A sky of black thunder—waterspouts, and birds. I heard them singing. Did you?"

"I did," came the reply. "It's something I can't understand. And yet," nudging his thumb at the mysterious apartment, "there isn't a thing in that room except a rug. We might have been a billion miles from San Francisco; perhaps on Mars or the Dog Star."

"Or we might have been dead," muttered Hal Watson; he was fumbling in his pocket; his hand came out with a paper. "It's just as Professor Holcomb promised. Here's that manuscript we got from Miss Stearns. Listen to the words of the great Doctor."

I desire something concrete; while my colleagues and others were pounding out tomes upon tomes of

55

wonderful sophistry, I have been working away at the screen of the Occult.

This is a proud moment.

I have succeeded. Tomorrow I shall bring you the fact and the substance. I have lifted the curtain and flooded it with the light of day. You shall have the fact for your senses. Tomorrow I shall explain it all. I shall deliver my greatest lecture, in which my whole life has come to focus. It is not spiritualism, nor sophistry. It is concrete fact and common sense. The subject of my lecture will be—"The Blind Spot."

"Well?" asked the detective.

"Just this," explained the other, "we know now that the lecture was never delivered. Something happened. The professor was never seen again. And we have the answer in there. What is it?"

"The old man called it the Occult," came the reply.

"To be sure. But he said also that it had nothing to do with spiritualism. So you see, we have been staring at a very natural law. By the way, did you notice the white substance of that dais?"

"What about it?"

"It was snow-white, remember? The same substance we found upstairs."

The detective whistled. "Do you think so?"

"I know it. And if it is, it will give us something to go on. Surely there is some connection."

"Search me," replied the detective. "Once in a while I have a feeling that I'm going to believe in ghosts. That fellow Senestro—"

"He was no phantom," announced Hal Watson. "He smoked cigarettes and purchased papers. He could talk and read English. Remember that. No, you're on the wrong track. We've bumped into something even greater."

"Maybe."

Hal Watson consulted his watch. "Let's go out and eat."

In another moment they were out on the steps, gazing down upon San Francisco Bay. The sun was setting; the shadows of the western mountains lay upon the inland water; far away along the crests of the Contra Costa hills the last rays lay like a crown of gold. The detective heaved a sigh of relief.

"Lord," he muttered, "this is surely a change. Dear old daylight! I feel like I had been on another planet."

A half hour later they were seated at a comfortable table, filled with substantial food—roast beef and dressing— followed by apple pie and all the trimmings. Things began to look natural again. Nevertheless:

"I can't get away from one thing," said Hal Watson. "We've been looking at some sort of law—natural phenomena. You represent the police—so we're protected on that side. But there is another—the scientific aspect of the case. This is a place for experts—real physicists of the first rank. Too bad we can't have some one tonight."

"But how does it come your father did not invite them in? Why his silence?"

That was a conundrum Hal could not answer; he thought it over, then:

"It makes no difference. His part is done. My duty lies in a different direction. Why should he die at the sight of this Senestro? That absolves me. Anyway, we can't do more tonight than watch. We'll go back and turn things over. Tomorrow we'll get busy."

"How about this Jimmy Fuillard, the lawyer? What did he know about the Spot?"

THE SPOT OF LIFE

That was something different. Hal Watson arose. Detective Flanning watched him enter a telephone booth; a minute later he stepped out.

"Well?" from the detective.

"They expect him back tonight," came the answer. "We'll get him in the morning. Let's see. Here's his card. If anything happens to me, look him up."

They paid the cashier, stepped into the street. Soon they were back at Chatterton Place looking across at the House of Mystery. The same gloom was in the air. The officer nodded.

"Too much for me," he said. "It's like walking through a shadow. It gets you."

They went up the steps, opened the door, turned on the lights. Both men stopped, listened. No sound—the silence was oppressive. The detective tiptoed back to the library, sat down under the reading lamp. Half mechanically, he began going through the drawers of the desk, digging out scraps of paper—mostly notes of a philosophical nature. Hal Watson began reading; he glanced up.

"Interesting in a way," he remarked, "but I don't think they will get us very far. These things, by their context, might have been written by my father. Hello! What's this?"

He was holding a sort of contract, brief but to the point, signed at the bottom by two names—Rhamda Avec and Chalmers C. Watson. It read:

Know ye. For the benefit of all concerned, we hereby agree and swear, by our conception of honor, never to divulge the secret of the Blind Spot, and we furthermore agree that, for the good of mankind, we shall do our utmost to keep the said Spot closed forever.

CHALMERS C. WATSON
RHAMDA AVEC.

58

THE SPOT OF LIFE

That was all. But it was enough. The men looked at each other. The detective nodded.

"Sounds nice," he said, "especially that part where it says for the good of mankind. Hal, my boy, I don't like it."

"Neither do I. However, this contract has nothing to do with me. Just the same, I would like to know what was at the bottom of their understanding."

The detective did not reply. He was sitting close by the desk, his glance roving around the room, finally stopping on the array of bookshelves. Suddenly he rose to his feet.

"Wait a minute," he commanded.

What was the matter? Something in the detective's tone announced an additional discovery. Hal Watson watched him running his hand along the line of shelves, stopping at a boxlike panel about four inches square. Flanning touched it with his fingers. He drew back.

"Come here, Watson. Put your hand on this."

Hal Watson had risen, holding up his right arm. A strange feeling ran through his fingers.

"It's cold," he muttered in an awed tone. "What is it?"

Flanning did not answer. Instead, he reached for his pocketknife, shoved it under the panel, pried it up. The piece of polished cedar gave way, laying bare the mortared boxing. Both men crowded up and peered inside. It was another white stone, set in an aluminum framework—a perfect mate to the one they had found upstairs!

X

THE WORLD MOVES

HERE WAS a tremendous fact. Whatever the potence of the Blind Spot, it had a foundation in natural law. Both men grasped the idea immediately. The detective grunted his pleasure.

"Now then," he said, "we're doing something. That old duffer was working a system. What do you think of it?"

Hal Watson had stepped closer; two feet away he could see its frozen light, gleaming softly. But why was it hidden inside the panel?

"Search me," he answered. "Why not look for more? Let's make another search."

But there was nothing to be found, although they kept up the search for hours. The detective finally became sleepy, gave up the hunt.

"Ghosts or no ghosts," he announced, "I'm all in. Hey ho!" with a yawn, "I'm going to hit the hay. You can sit up and watch. So long, Watson. Call me if you see a spook."

And with scarcely a warning he stretched himself out in one of the bedrooms. Watson had never seen a man fall asleep so quickly. It was almost hypnotic.

Yet, strangely enough, he himself had never been wider awake. He stood by the bed, listening.

Listening to what?

There was, of course, the breathing of the detective; but just the same, he sensed a queer dread. It was out of his experience, totally foreign. Watson opened the door and peered into the next room.

Silence!

THE SPOT OF LIFE

But what a silence! Here there were none of the minor trivialities that buzz through the air of ordinary life—not even the whir of an insect. And besides, it was night—with all its suspense and suggestion. But why was there no no sound from the streets? Surely there should be something—a rumble if nothing else.

Then—the thought flashed through his mind. Here was isolation—one that could not be natural. Perhaps—

Next instant he was at the outside door, turning the knob, and stepping onto the steps leading to the sidewalk. A cab was turniing the corner of the street; some one was laughing; a girl's voice rose in shrill crescendo. Down below twinkled the lights of San Francisco—blinking to the roar of metropolitan traffic. Here was life and sound, joy and the thrill of living! Puzzled, he stepped back through the doorway.

The sounds had ceased; silence enshrouded him.

And all within the space of a few short feet. The door was wide open; he could still see the lights—but that was all. The thing was beyond reason. A choking sensatior. rose in his throat.

He had found a soundproof curtain, invisible but real, cutting him off from earthly realities. Half stunned and still doubting, he stepped out to make a second test.

It was the same as before. The house of the Blind Spot was an entity in itself, isolated in mystery. Puzzled and uncertain, Hal Watson closed the door and returned to the library. He sat down at the table, trying to think.

But that was a difficult thing to do; too much had happened; the events of the day flew past in a hashed-up reverie. Nothing was clear—facts were mixed and out of sequence. Still—here he was in the house of the Blind Spot!

Surely there should be an explanation. He thought again of the jewel upstairs, of its strange materialization; and the accompanying explosion. And there was also this stone, which they had discovered in the hidden panel. He stepped over to examine it.

For a moment he was fascinated by its glow and color—and its frigidity. Cold as an iceberg! Yet it gave off a current. It seemed alive—sparkling with some unknown power. Absently, he held up his hand, watched the weirdly-cold white light. Then—

He became aware that the fleshy part of his hand had become invisible, and that he was looking at the bones of his skeleton. Here was another fact; the stone, whatever its substance, was giving off a ray.

What could it mean?

The simplest answer was that it might be a part of a network of similar stones, each one functioning in its relative niche. There ought to be others. The fact that he and the detective had failed in the previous search meant nothing. He was sure he was right.

Suddenly the inspiration dawned.

He remembered having seen a steel tape in the desk. He fished it out. After that he opened the door that led into the room of the Blind Spot, tossed the end of the line to the center of the rug and measured the distance to the panel. Sixteen feet, six inches!

So much to go on; but what would he do next?

His idea was simple. Upstairs there was another stone with an undoubted affinity for the one in front of him. But before going up, he looked in again at the detective, noticed his coma-like sleep and posture—spread out in a figure of a cross. Perhaps he was dead! No—his heart was beating; the pulse was strong!

So far, so good.

Hal Watson started for the corkscrew stairway, ascending

slowly, until he had reached the secret door leading to the laboratory. He stopped and listened. There was no sound—nothing but that void-like silence. Softly he tiptoed into the room, shut the door.

Things were just as he had left them, scattered about the asbestos covered table and on the floor. The shelves were filled with apparatus; over in the corner was the glass tumbler containing the snow stone, the ice clinging to the sides—with the jewel in the center. But just for the present, Hal Watson was interested in the room.

He was fascinated most of all by the broken pieces of fused instruments. Piece by piece he gathered up the metal scraps in an effort at identification. But in the end he gave it up. He turned his attention to the other contents of the room.

"Let me see," he muttered. "We have two stones. The other one was hidden in a panel. But this one was not even manufactured. Perhaps— Wait a minute! Down below the distance was sixteen feet, six inches. I wonder how far this room is from the center.".

It was purely conjecture; nevertheless, it was something. Hal Watson returned to the head of the stairs, glanced down, estimating the height and approximate position of the laboratory. Then he returned and sat down by the carpenter's bench.

More computation; but all to no purpose.

The best he could do was to gaze idly about the room, at the shelves and array of test tubes. There were no panels and no visible wiring. Behind him was the work bench, cluttered with bits of wood, hammers, planes, and a keyhole saw.

Quite by accident he noticed that the teeth of the saw blade were covered with specks of reddish dust; which, of course, amounted to nothing. But a moment later when he began rummaging through the wooden pieces of odds and ends, he ran across another discovery—a mitred box of cedar, possibly eight inches square, with bits of aluminum casting screwed into the sides as if to act as the body base for some inside setting.

Here was something at least.

Curious, he picked it up, turned it over, examined the workmanship, glancing over at the teeth of the keyhole saw. His mind was wandering, searching for details. Half by chance, he touched the ice containing the frozen crystal; but drew back with a grunt of dismay. It was colder than he could believe; and like the jewel on the lower floor, it gave forth a peculiar glow. Yet there was no reaction.

Hal Watson was convinced that he was on the right track. The dust on the saw blade fascinated him; he kept wondering. And just then he glanced at the baseboard along the wall where a streak of dust cluttered the floor. He stooped over, scraped some of it in his fingers, brought it to the light. It was sawdust!

Sawdust!

It was a little thing, but one that led a long way. Two and two make four! The particles in his hand and those on the blade were identical. Evidently from some recent job. Hal Watson glanced from the baseboard to the side wall.

At first he could see nothing; the light was dim; but after a minute he noticed a detail along the woodwork—a slight depression coated with varnish. Still guessing, he reached up with his knife, began prying. The wood gave way, revealing a pocket panel about nine inches square.

Could it be another setting for a stone?

At least there was no harm trying it out. Carefully, he reached out with a piece of cotton waste, caught hold of the frozen tumbler, lifted it up and placed it within the half finished panel.

THE SPOT OF LIFE

A curious thing happened.

First of all, the jewel gave off flashes of cold light; the room became charged with sultry magnetism. The silence was deathlike, oppressive.

That was the first reaction. The second was a sensation of high motion. The room whirled, was lost to view; lights flashed before his eyes—dancing, twisting, fantastic, and then as suddenly, bursting into a sheen of snow whiteness.

Hal Watson hung on. He remembered but one thought— whatever the end might be, he must retain consciousness. But that was beyond him. His mind reeled. Then—the light broke into the prosaic reality of fact and substance. He was standing in the center of the laboratory; the place was just as it should be—with a single exception; the frozen jewel had fallen out of the panel and was lying on the floor at his feet.

XI

THE BELL

HAL WATSON was the victim of strange reactions. He felt numb all over, his mind blurred, his body was sick. A peculiar nausea settled upon him. He barely managed to crawl to a chair. Vaguely he noted his surroundings—formed conjectures.

The jewel!

Ah, that was it! He began piecing things together. The stone had exerted a peculiar reaction; perhaps it was the key to the Blind Spot.

But was it? And even if it were, would he have the courage to try it again? Suddenly he remembered Flanning asleep in the room below. He wondered whether the detective had been caught within the weird transition. Drunkenly, he stood up and staggered for the crooked stairs, clutching the wall as he felt his way down. It seemed an age; but finally he reached the lower floor, dropped onto a chesterfield. The world suddenly went black again. The next thing he knew, some one was bending over him, shaking his arm.

"Watson! Watson!" came a faraway voice. "Wake up! What's happened?"

After that, the voice died away; footsteps sounded from the kitchen; he heard a noise like running water; the man returned and was thrusting a tumbler to his lips. The water revived him; he looked up.

"Did you see it, Flanning—I mean hear it? Or were you asleep?"

"Tell me."

Hal Watson sat up; his memory returned; he went into detail. The detective nodded grimly:

66

THE SPOT OF LIFE

"I didn't hear it; and I didn't see it. But if I ever had a nightmare, it was just before you staggered downstairs. I would have sworn there was some one in the room where I was sleeping. Then—I came out here and found you. And now that I have got you, I'm going to take you down town, and let this place go hang. We can come back to-morrow."

But Hal Watson was not to be convinced; he sat with his head between his hands, thinking.

"Do you know," he said, "I'd like to know more about my grandfather. He had a lot on the ball, and I've got a hunch that he solved Death!"

"Huh?"

"It isn't impossible, is it? Life is a thing that exists; and as long as it is a reality, somebody's going to find its law."

"Yeah? Well, what about these stones? Looks to me too much like trickery—television, perhaps."

"That may be. But I don't think so. Haven't you noticed that there isn't a bit of radio equipment in this building? No, Professor Holcomb wasn't playing with television. He promised a day greater than the coming of Columbus. He solved the Occult—the mystery of Death!"

"Come on," snapped the other, "let's get out of here. We can come back tomorrow in plain daylight. We'll get them scientists you speak about and let them go after it according to Hoyle. Come on, Hal—"

The detective stopped short as if the words had been frozen; the atmosphere had become charged—loaded with suspense. The silence was unearthly. Hal Watson had risen from his chair, listening.

"Strange," he whispered. "Flanning, there's some one moving about in this room!"

"Mebbe it's the same guy who was standing over my

head in that nightmare," grunted the detective. "Come on. Let's go."

Instead, Hal Watson walked to the door of the Blind Spot room, pulled it open. The place was empty. A weird shadow streaked along the wall, twisting and turning grotesquely, then it disappeared. He stepped inside, listened. Behind him he could see the detective standing beside the pendulum of a great wall clock. The thing had been dead before; but now it was moving. Strange.

And stranger still was the ghostlike exaggeration of its unearthly tick. It was ringing like a bell:

Ding! Dong! Ding! Dong!

The detective was waiting; he had pulled out a cigar, was lighting a match. His lips moved, but Hal could not hear his voice. Then—Hal Watson came to his senses. The sound he heard was not the clock. It was a bell—far off, yet close at hand ringing like a tocsin, clarion in its distinctness—direct.

Ding dong! Ding dong! Ding dong!

And still the detective waited; his face was blank. His lips moved in silence. Hal Watson stepped through the door. The reverberations of the mystic bell had suddenly ceased.

"What's the matter?" asked the impatient Flanning.

The younger man beckoned. "Step inside this door," he answered. "There now. Listen. Do you hear anything?"

Ding dong! Ding dong! Ding dong!

"What is it?"

"That's for us to find out!" came the answer. "Can't you see, Flanning? The same curtain of silence that surrounds the outside of the building, shuts off this room. So there must be a focus within a focus. This apartment is a sort of holy of holies! Something is going on in this spot right where we are standing."

The bell suddenly stopped; the silence that ensued was

68

even deeper than it had been before. The men strained their ears, listening. Hal Watson stepped to the door, mopped his face.

"I'd give a leg," he said, "if it would come daylight. Flanning, I guess you're right. We'd better go."

But Flanning was already gone!

XII

INTO THE SPOT

HAL CROSSED the library, stepped to the front door; for a moment he forgot about his companion. San Francisco lay below, a mass of lights gleaming under the stars.

His own world! So near and yet so far! It was full of actuality—and life. And he had been looking at—death! The thought startled him; he drew back, caught the door in his left hand. What had become of Sam Flanning? He glanced up and down the street; the man was nowhere in sight.

Strange!

Perhaps, after all, Flanning had not preceded him. He returned to the hall, shut the door, looked around. There was naught but the ghostly light and the statuette of Rodin's "Thinker" in the far corner. The deadly silence reeked mystery. He called out:

"Flanning!"

But there was only the clamor of his own voice. The silence settled like a fog. Hal Watson could not understand. If Flanning had not gone out, he was surely in the house. But where?

"Oh, Flanning!"

Again that explosion of sound, followed by the silence of isolation. He started for the stairway; but just then he thought of something else. Perhaps Flanning was in the room of the Blind Spot. That would account for his not hearing.

But again he was mistaken. The apartment was empty. There was nothing in the room but the rug and a piece or two of apparatus he and Flanning had brought down from upstairs.

THE SPOT OF LIFE

An awful suspicion clutched at his consciousness; could it be that Flanning had ventured inside and had been caught up by the Blind Spot? But Flanning was no fool. Perhaps after all, he had preceded him to the street.

Still, Hal could not leave; he was working along the side wall, clutching with his outstretched fingers, waiting for he knew not what. The air had become magnetic again; there came a slight rustling, like wind whispering around a corner. Something was going on—right where he was standing.

Ah! There it was!

A tiny dot of blue simmered in the ceiling, flickered, disappeared. But along with its presence came a recurrence of the previous phenomenon, the clanging of a bell from the distance!

Ding dong! Ding dong! Ding dong!

Intuition warned Hal Watson; he was ready for the Blind Spot. He stole up slowly, surely. Then it came again—a queer, crackling sound, dropping out of nothing and materializing in a needle point upon the ceiling.

A speck of blue flame!

That's what it was at first—the bluest blue of the spectrum, unholy and alive— the scintillations of a million jewels focused into one. The color of life and death, concentrated! Hal Watson was frozen, his body flattened against the wall, waiting.

The dot changed color, dropping into a livid ultramarine, growing, spreading out and suddenly turning into a white string of incandescence. Like a living thing it pulsed here and there, reaching about the room, bulging and finally bursting at the center.

A ball of mystic fire—giving forth—a man! The Bar Senestro!

Hal Watson knew him in an instant. Every detail tallied— the reddish hair, the cruel handsome face, the splendid

71

body. Even the eyes and the lips that spoke, but uttered no sound.

It came as a blur to Hal Watson. First there was a livid picture, then a man rushing at him. Watson was fighting for his life, striking, dancing and dodging about that string of incandescence, pounding flesh on flesh and taking blows in return.

Who was this Bar Senestro? The fellow was a fiend—no man could fight better. The room turned into a whirlpool —a seething mass of action. But Hal Watson could not stand it forever. He was done.

No, not done! Something had happened. First of all, he felt himself lifted up, thrown, landing on his feet like a cat. Then—he was free, looking back.

It was Flanning! The detective had come through the door, tackling like a catapult. The Bar Senestro was off his feet, rolling over. That was all.

There came a blur of bluish light—and a sense of tremendous vibration. The world changed, passed into nothingness. Hal Watson lost consciousness and fell down; his face against a snow-white substance; his arms spread out, head-on through the Blind Spot.

XIII

A CALL FOR HELP!

WHAT WAS it all about?

Flanning, the detective, was never to forget that crowded moment when he came rushing into the room to find the tangle of arms and legs fighting in and out through the Blind Spot. It was like a flash. He could see Hal Watson, rolling over from a blow to the jaw, staggering into the line of incandescence with the Bar Senestro driving in for a swift finish. The next instant he had gone into action himself—making a healthy tackle and knocking his man against the wall, pinning him hard, only to have the fellow spin out of his grasp and send him into the center of the room.

For a moment the world went into a whirl, a catch-as-catch-can struggle of life and death—throat throttling, short-arm punches to the pit of the stomach, no blows barred. But Flanning was no longer in his prime; he was matched against youth; his wind vanished; something happened. The last he knew, he was being tossed against the side wall—the world was full of music; a bell was donging its rhythm through a void. All was black!

The next Flanning knew he was alone, propped up in a corner, his clothes torn and his face battered. Had he gone through a sausage mill he could not have looked worse. His feet were still; his body swaying. He clung to the wall and fumbled his way to the kitchen. Soon he had his head under a faucet, bathing out the cobwebs. After a good toweling, he sought a mirror.

He was a pretty sight. One tooth was missing, an eye blacked, his nose swollen. Yet he was not sorry; at least, he had had a real chance at the mystery of the Blind Spot. It was material—flesh and blood, human! Still—and then a dreadful truth dawned:

Hal Watson was gone!

The whole picture came rushing back. He recalled that he had left his companion on the doorstep and had wandered upstairs to the laboratory, where he had picked up the snow-white jewel, carrying it over towards a window near the unfinished panel. Suddenly there had come a flash, followed immediately by the noise downstairs. He had rushed below—and opened the door of the Blind Spot room. Then—

He had seen the last of Hal Watson. Before he could understand, he was in a fight for his own life. It was the Senestro! The name rang in his ears, slipped to his tongue.

"I wonder," he muttered. "He must have knocked me cold. What a licking! Mebbe he's in this house. I'd like another crack at him."

He felt of his automatic, wondered why he had not used it; and whether, if he had done so, it would have had any effect. Clutching it in his hand he returned to the room. The place was empty. His thoughts raced back, and then he remembered the words:

"We've got to see Jimmy Fuillard. Here's his card. If anything happens to me, don't fail to look him up immediately."

At the same instant, he felt of the pasteboard in his pocket, pulled it out, read:

JIMMY FUILLARD
Attorney at Law
1001 Balbee Bldg.   San Francisco

Detective Flanning turned it over and over; shoved it back in his pocket. Certainly it was worth trying.

THE SPOT OF LIFE

After that he worked through the house, examining every room. But there was not a sign of an occupant. Finally he opened the outside door and gazed down into the city. Old San Francisco was still sleeping, although it was morning. Beautiful—splendid, perfect. For a moment he stood spellbound—like a man wakening from a dream. Surely it could not be real. He was right here at 288 Chatterton, where—

A light flickered in the house next door—the one where he had met the old lady. For a moment it glared weakly, dimmed out, and then flared up again. He heard a sound like a pan rattling. It made him think of breakfast. Also it brought up another thought. He noticed telephone wires running to the dwelling. Why not call up Jimmy Fuillard? That brought him back to the card for additional information. Fortunately it gave two phone numbers—one for business, the other a home number.

Detective Flanning took a chance. He knocked on the door where he had seen the light. The old lady he had met the day before answered the call. She seemed frightened; but still she understood.

"Oh," she said, when Flanning asked for the phone, "did something happen? Oh, sir, I wanted to stop you. It is terrible. That place—the Blind Spot! I don't know what it is. But—whom do you want to call sir?"

Flanning showed her the card; he read the name. Whereupon he was in for another surprise. The old lady clutched his arm.

"You don't mean Jimmy Fuillard. What—oh, sir! Is Jimmy mixed up in this terrible business? Tell me!"

Here was a clue with a vengeance; Flanning held the card between his thumb and finger.

"Who is Jimmy Fuillard?" he asked. "Do you know him? Come, mother, tell me."

75

THE SPOT OF LIFE

The old lady was terribly frightened; she clutched him tighter, breathing her words:

"He is my nephew. And such a good boy. He has been here many times. But he always laughed. Oh, sir, what has happened?"

Detective Flanning had placed his call; he could hear the weird early morning ring on the other end. A sleepy voice finally answered:

"Hello! Hello! Who's calling?"

"This is Flanning—a detective. Is this Jimmy Fuillard, the attorney?"

"Yes."

"Pardon me for such a call. This is tremendously important. You have a friend named Hal Watson. He has been trying to get you all night. He—"

"Hal—Hal Watson. Say, listen. What's happened? You mean Professor Watson's son? The football player? Where are you?"

"I'm up here at your aunt's house on Chatterton Place. I—"

He was drowned by the voice on the other end.

"You mean—Hey! I've read the papers. It's—it's that damned Blind Spot. Say—don't tell me a word over the wire. I'll be up as soon as wheels can bring me. And don't go back into that house until I get there."

Flanning could hear the click of the phone. He turned to the old lady standing by his side.

"Oh, sir," she was saying, "Jimmy will know. He always laughed; but he is a splendid boy. And he understands about law and all; them things that keep people befuddled. He was educated in a college and can explain everything— even this terrible Blind Spot."

XIV

JIMMY FUILLARD

JIMMY FUILLARD, the attorney, was young, hale and hearty, good looking; but most important, he was the nephew of the queer little old lady, Selena Whitcomb, a friend and fraternity brother of Hal Watson. Naturally his association led him into the Blind Spot.

First of all, there was his aunt, who was one of the sweetest little women in the world, and the most superstitious, a lover of the weird and the unusual, who would not have traded her abode on the uncanny street for the grandest palace in the world. It was her greatest pride; as often as her nephew came over to visit, she would take him out and point to the border of soft shadow. And Jimmy Fuillard, prosaic and skeptical, could feel it.

The world would change, a clutching tremor would seize his heart. Always there was that alternation of sunshine and fog—a glimpse of the Pacific or a rush of gray mist along his feet as it scooted out over the bay. But being young and full of confidence, he blamed it all on the location.

But not his Aunt Selena. Hers was a tale of ghosts and weird happenings. Her mind reeked fairy tales and witches—strange unaccountable miracles that brought back the dead. Jimmy Fuillard got a kick from her stories. Firally, she had breathed her greatest confidence.

She was actually living next door to the House of the Blind Spot!

It was terrible, the home of the uncanny, abode of spirits. And there was a great deal more. She spoke of hearing the tolling of a spirit bell, ringing from a far-off heaven.

THE SPOT OF LIFE

Her accomplishment grew from day to day, and at each telling, her fancy would add on a new color.

The nephew had heard the recounting many times. However, one day he ran across something that brought him up with a jump. He happened to have a class under a certain Doctor Connor—Philosophy 2B; and one afternoon while walking across the campus, accidentally ran the conversation into the Occult. He told of his aunt and her masterpiece—the Blind Spot. The reaction of the doctor was startling; it went back as far as the days of Professor Holcomb and the famous lecture. He told a story.

The things had become real. Fuillard turned investigator. Next time he was over in San Francisco, he climbed to the uncanny street for a good look. But he did not tell his aunt what had occurred. He still went on with his teasing, until suddenly the door of the ghost house had opened and a man stepped out. The old lady pointed

"There!" she spoke testily. "There is the man who lives in the house. Look at him and see. Am I wrong?"

Beyond the fact that the gentleman was a neighbor, Jimmy Fuillard had never before paid him the least attention. But on this occasion there was a difference. The man was tall, of Eurasian cast, and old. As he turned to lock the door, Fuillard caught a closer glimpse. There was something illusive—an expression that defied scrutiny; the man might have been any age at all.

Jimmy Fuillard questioned his aunt carefully, hoping to get down to some sensible fact; but when she insisted upon her rumors and old lady's lore, he decided to forget it.

That is—for a while.

After graduating, Fuillard had taken up the profession of law. Two years passed and then, one night, he encountered the Rhamda Avec again—this time in a restaurant.

It was at Tony's—just off Powell Street. He was finish-

78

ing an evening meal when two men entered the room, took a seat opposite him. One of them was the mysterious stranger, the other Professor Chalmers C. Watson. That brought Fuillard back to the story of the Blind Spot and his conversation with Doctor Connor. He knew Professor Watson to be the son-in-law of the great Doctor Holcomb. The two men were conversing in low tones; and they held plenty of respect for each other. What was the connection?

Then, about two weeks later, he ran into Hal Watson at a social function and brought up the question of the Blind Spot, but just as he got going, some fool switched the conversation into a gale of laughter.

That ended that. The football season came around, and Hal Watson was in training. Fuillard had departed to the wilds of Del Norte County on a bear hunt, where an accident had kept him from the great college classic. He was at Crescent City when he picked up papers. First there was an account of the game; and second, the story of the Blind Spot.

The Blind Spot!

The thing had become a menacing reality—a mystery that approached murder. Fuillard was convinced; his first act on reaching San Francisco was to call up the Watson home in Berkeley, but Hal was out. Then he turned in and slept, to be awakened early in the morning by some one calling. A detective was at his Aunt Selena's on Chatterton Place; and he was talking about Hal Watson. In a few minutes Jimmy Fuillard was driving full speed for his encounter with the Blind Spot.

After telephoning, Detective Flanning sat down on an old chair; his hands clutching the sides of his head. He needed thought, plenty of it. Everything—details, sequence, facts—had become hopelessly confused; and on top of all else,

79

there was that one truth pounding its way through his consciousness:

Hal Watson was gone—caught by the Blind Spot!

The old lady puttered at the stove, cooking; always her voice repeating:

"I knew it. I knew it. But no one would listen. I wonder what they'll say next? Dear me, this is a wicked world. There now, my good man, don't worry. Everything will come out all right."

Surely, she was a good old soul, the kind to love and trust. Ten minutes went by, and then there came a sound outside—a car drawing up at the curb. Steps at the door; a young man walked into the room.

"Well?" he asked. "What happened?"

Flanning looked up; the introduction was of a sudden sort; his battered face gave fair warning. Next minute he was explaining all he knew. Jimmy Fuillard whistled. The old lady nodded her head.

"I knew it. I knew it," she repeated. "And I told you, Jimmy, long ago. Dear me! And they's some that say they can't believe in ghosts. And right here where we have the Blind Spot."

However, she did not forget to serve the breakfast; the detective did the best he could with his swollen jaw; Jimmy needed no help. After he had eaten, he shoved back his plate.

"All right," he said, "now we'll go over and take a look. Auntie, do you want to come along?"

He had confidence to brace up the detective—the quality of youth and courage. Yet it was somewhat diminished when they climbed the steps of the building, stopped at the door and gazed down at the city, where the stir of a new day was filling the air. Over in the east the rim of the sun was cresting the hills of Contra Costa. The detective opened the door and motioned for Jimmy Fuillard to walk inside. The other did just that—turned around and was caught by the veil of silence. His face dropped.

"What is it?" came his question.

But the old lady was emphatic.

"Just as I said. Just as I said—always! Now then, Jimmy Fuillard, you can laugh if you want to."

Strange to relate, she was the least perturbed of the three; she entered the library, cast an appraising eye along the books, and opened the door to the Blind Spot.

Jimmy Fuillard was right behind her, examining the walls and looking up at the panel. His face had whitened.

"Notice anything?" asked the detective.

"Yes and no," came the puzzled answer. "There's nothing here, and yet—"

The other nodded. "That's the whole thing! Yes and no! But if you had seen what I have, you wouldn't doubt."

Fuillard did not reply; already the weirdness and isolation of the house had caught him; he held his breath. No sound! The old lady turned back from the door; her lips thin and compressed; she jerked a crooked finger in the direction of the Blind Spot.

"It's, it's—in there, isn't it?"

There was no denying her tone; she was shaken. Jimmy Fuillard had stepped past her into the room. Flanning walked behind.

"Right there in the center," said the detective. "A spot of light in the ceiling—it drops like a string of incandescence. It comes and it goes."

"You have seen all this?"

"Exactly. In the center of that room. Say—where are you going? Don't do that!"

Jimmy Fuillard had stepped from the wall, straight across

the floor, stopping under the exact spot where the dot would appear. For a moment he was tremendously interested. He studied the height.

"About eight feet. I should say. And the floor is made of Tennessee oak."

He scraped the rug with his foot and drew it back. "But there's nothing here. Did you look in the cellar?"

"Everywhere," came the answer. "The only things we discovered were two strange jewels, one upstairs and the other in a panel in the wall of the library."

"I'm going to take a look."

They started for the stairs, followed by Aunt Selena, who, now that she had the opportunity, was overlooking nothing. Yet there was no denying her frightened appearance. At the laboratory she stopped and looked inside.

"Dear me," she muttered. "Of all the places. He must have been in league with Satan himself. Jimmy, I'm right. This house is full of ghosts. It's—it isn't holy. Can't you feel it?"

The men left her, entered the room; once again the little laboratory got a thorough going over. Finally Jimmy Fuillard picked up the snow stone, examined it, and looked at his watch.

If you don't mind," he said, "I'm going to take this to a friend of mine. He's a specialist. He'll tell me."

Down at the first floor again he glanced at the other jewel and started to pry it with his knife; suddenly he drew back—a look of amazement in his eyes. Then he touched it again. This time he slipped back and gazed up.

"I wonder what it is," he said. "Do you know? I never had such a queer feeling in my life. It isn't electricity, yet—"

"Radio-active," answered Flanning simply. "That's what Hal Watson says."

The other shook his head. "No, that wouldn't account for

82

it. There's something else— This Rhamda, whoever he was, knew something. Honestly, from what I've seen, it looks like he was calling the dead. Anyhow, I'm not going to take a chance on that stone. This frozen one is enough."

He picked up the asbestos wrapping and stepped through the door calling his aunt, warning the detective to await his return. A moment later he had turned the corner and was heading into the city. Finally, to speed things, he called a taxi and was driven to a three-story structure on Turk Street. The lower floor carried the name, J. C. Couland— Wholesale Jeweler. Upstairs were the simple words, California Chemists. Without a word he entered, walked to the rear of the building. A lean, cadaverous expert looked up alertly.

"Hello. What you got?"

"Where's Fred? Call him down."

Whereupon he placed the mysterious asbestos wrapping on the table. The cadaverous one looked over his spectacles, whistled into a tube and rose to his long lean legs. His hand went out, removing the asbestos from the stone. The man jerked back in amazement.

"What the—" he exclaimed. "Say—of all things. Well, this is the—" Then with a decisive gesture he caught the speaking tube: "Say, Fred, come on down here. Here's something for your wisdom."

A man appeared at the door; a stubby little fellow with a round face and abstract eyes; stepped over.

"Vass iss?" he demanded. "None of your funny jokes, I hope. This is my busy day." He had spotted the stone, clinging with vaporish ice upon the counter. "By golly, where did you get it?"

"What is it, Fred?" from the lean one.

"How should I know? By golly, dot don't look natural, does it? A jool mid ice clinging over its whiskers. Funny!"

83

THE SPOT OF LIFE

He pulled out a steel rod and turned the object over. For a moment he studied, then he called for a glass, focused it in his eyes and began another scrutiny. Finally:

"Where'd you get it? Dot's a stone; but nothing like any w'at I ever seen."

Jimmy Fuillard explained what he could. Immediately the pudgy little man was all interest.

"So!" he exclaimed. "So, I know all about dot house. I mean I heard of it once before. Long time ago a friend of mine tell me about another stone that wasn't natural. Just like dis one, only different. A young feller named Harry Wendell came along with a stone and asked my friend what it was. It was lighter than air. You get dot! But my friend didn't lie. Dot stone slipped out of his fingers and hit the ceiling. Dot was against all law, you know. But the young feller wouldn't let my friend keep it for experiment; he kept it till it killed him."

"Killed him?"

"You bet. Up in dot house on Chatterton Place. I didn't see it; but I haf a friend whose father used to be agent for dot property. He—"

"Would you mind taking me to this friend?"

"Sure. Vait till I get my coat. Und I'm going to see the house where this stone comes from."

A short time later, Jimmy Fuillard and his companions were sitting in a real estate office down town listening to a story—at least the shadow of one. A young fellow of about thirty-four years with a prosperous come-on appearance looked up from his desk.

"Sure," he was saying, "I know what you are talking about. My father had that place years ago. And say, was he scared? I'll tell you, he was. I've heard him recite his tale many a time. The place was hoodooed, smeared with death. He'd

84

rent it to a man and the man would disappear. Then a young fellow about twenty-five years old got a lease—and started to go downhill. It was like a disease.

"In less than six months that boy didn't weigh more than one hundred and fifty—and still weakening. He was like a man hypnotized; going, going—alseep, and finally he wasn't more than a skeleton. And when he disappeared another fine young fellow by the name of Harry Wendell took his place. Same fate! Whatever it was, the thing ate into their souls—and snuffed them up. But if I remember rightly, this Harry Wendell purchased the place. Dad was glad to get rid of it."

"Know anything more?"

The young man shook his head. "That's all except there was some sort of flurry a few days ago. The police looked it over and backed out. Called it all bunk—and nonsense. Maybe they were scared. Why?"

XV

THE WARNING

JIMMY FUILLARD had heard enough; he backed away with his companion. As they were getting into the taxi, he asked the German:

"What did you think about it?"

"W'at can I think until I look at the house? I think right now there's a monkey business. Yet, this fellow tells the truth. I heard him talk before. How did those young fellers die? Answer me dot?"

At the top of the hill they stopped; Jimmy paid the driver; he explained to his companion:

"I want you to walk across the street where you can get the benefit of the whole thing. There now. Notice the sun shining? Out here you feel natural. Now, then, we'll cross over."

Again the strange sensation seized them; indefinite to be sure, but not to be mistaken. The German sniffed cautiously, and true to his training walked back and repeated the performance. He noted the distance from the building—about two hundred feet.

When they had gained the steps Jimmy threw open the door and allowed his companion the sensation of silence. Again the German performed a calculation, moving in and out to make sure. Each time there was the full sweep of the city's racket on the outside and silence within the screen.

"All right," he said simply. "Now we go into the house. You say there iss one more stone? I want for see it."

The detective had come forward, was introduced.

"Anything happen?" asked Jimmy:

"All quiet on the Potomac," Flanning replied. "The old Spot is slumbering. But it's still there."

THE SPOT OF LIFE.

The German nodded; removed one pair of spectacles and put on another. First of all he looked at the statue in the corner. After that, he passed into the other room, stopped with evident admiration while he gazed at the books.

"By golly," he mumbled, "you say dis Rhamda vas-hiss-name have dis library, eh? Vell, he vas no fool. You can take dot for a start. Now, vere is dis Spot?"

Detective Flanning opened the door, pointed. Already he could feel the cool assurance of the valiant little German. The fellow held no fear—no superstition.

And yet, there was still the weird isolation that Flanning and Hal had noticed the night before. The squat little chemist stood still, listening. The detective pointed to the center of the room and told how Jimmy Fuillard had walked across.

"Like a fool," came the answer. "No, I don't vant to do dot. For why should I stick my head in the cannon? Better first find out about der law. But it ain't ghosts."

"What is it?"

The other shrugged his shoulders; he turned to Detective Flanning.

"Mebbe the old professor was right in his speech about dot Blind Spot. I read it in the paper. He said it would be the greatest day since Columbus. You bet."

Had they gone over the city with a fine tooth comb, they could not have picked up a better man than Frederick Van Tassel. Here was a level head—unafraid, emotionless, scientific. Already Flanning was picking up his spirits. The little fellow had turned from the Blind Spot, shut the door.

"Now," he said, "I vant for look at the other stone. Oh, I see. Now get me a chair. Here, you better keep this wrapped-up stone as far away as you can. Now then."

Slowly he boosted himself up, peering at the setting inside the panel, and finally bringing up his hand. For several moments he kept watching, never speaking. Finally he climbed down. Fuillard had expected him to pry out the paneled stone.

"No," the German said, "we disturb nothing. Why should we? This room is full of phenomena. So first we will see them same phenomena. Otherwise mebbe we will be electrocuted."

"Electricity?"

"How do I know? Everything is electric at the bottom. Vibration—ions, protons, nuclei—all just a humble-jumble to keep man guessing. W'at is electricity? No man knows. He sees it. He uses it. He feels it. But dot iss all."

He kept moving; as soon as he had satisfied himself about the panel stone he started for the stairs; climbing slowly and methodically, counting the steps and taking a mental measurement. Once inside the laboratory he sat down, his short little legs barely touching the floor.

"Where did you find the stone?" he asked at last. "Put it in the exact spot. I mean where you found it last. All right, now, leave it there."

Certainly he was a man of few words; his eyes roved up and down, crossways and back. At last he explained:

"Everything must be left just as it was—dot's the way we want it. Sure, the stones is mystery—but the phenomena are more important. I want to figure them out. Mebbe we'll get some more."

Fuillard and the detective were getting a glimpse of the wonderful difference in human beings; where they had been all excitement and emotion, this man could see nothing but experiment. At last the chemist was satisfied: he started for the stairs. At the bottom he caught Sam Flanning by the shoulder.

"More better you go to bed," he advised. "I don't think

we'll have anything exciting, for a while yet, anyway. And you need sleep."

There was truth in that. Flanning sought the bed in the spare room and in spite of his wounds was soon wrapped in slumber. Jimmy Fuillard walked to the house next door. The German kept on with his figures, measuring the rooms, one by one, and even the cellar. Finally, he did even more than that—he stepped outside, walked across the street, and found the extreme border of the weirdness, noting his calculation in a memorandum.

When the attorney returned, they met on the steps. The German conducted him to the library. He held up his pencil suggestively.

"Here," he said, "iss w'at I find so far. For instance, first, we have concentric rings of influence—the first approximately two hundred feet from the Blind Spot. Und another a little different, about two hundred feet—I mean the radius, you understand?—und finally from the door, another at about twenty-four feet. And the stones both at variant angles."

"What do you make of it?"

The German held up his hands. "Give me a chance. I hafn't made anything. I'm only trying. But those rings mean a lot. There iss magnetism or something like it, setting up a sphere of vibratory contact. The farther you get inside, the less you feel like a real man. And dot stone"—indicating the one in the library panel—"isn't a stone at all."

"What is it?"

"I don't know. But she's the king business of it all. I would call it a sort of key. But listen, Mr. Fuillard. Did they really watch the jewel upstairs grow from nothing?"

"I guess they did. The whole thing sounds impossible, but if one is true, the rest must follow."

THE SPOT OF LIFE

The German blinked, looking straight ahead. "If I didn't know better, I would call it all damn monkey-business. *Ya!* But I see dot stone and I have got to believe. It ain't miracle because dot ain't common sense. It's natural; but what kind of natural you call this?"

"Search me," said the attorney. "It's slightly off my line. But I'd give all I ever hope to possess to solve this Blind Spot. I can feel it. Huh! It gives me the creeps—Listen!"

They were sitting close by the door, facing each other. Something stirred inside—slowly, mysteriously, like a cloth dragged across the floor. Instantly the tense atmosphere deepened into a voidlike suspense. Jimmy Fuillard slipped nervously from his chair; but the German stepped forward; he caught the door handle, pulled it open. The silence that had been so maddening before was swept away by a vibration of musical rhythm, ethereal and thrilling. Then—a sound like a bell—far off, ringing a clarion of strange warning. Ding, dong! Ding, dong! Ding, dong!

But there was not a thing in sight—the room was exactly as it had been. Frederick Van Tassel crept along the wall, waiting. Fuillard kept by the door. The sound continued: Ding, dong! Ding, dong! Ding, dong!—dying at length into vibration and at last into silence. But just at the final instant, a tiny dot focused in the center of the ceiling —a fiery intense blue, flashing intermittently and dying out. That was all.

The little chemist had seen enough; he returned, picked up a chair and placed it in the doorway. Fuillard was mopping his forehead.

"Well," asked the attorney in a whisper, "what was it? Now I'll believe in Aunt Selena's ghosts. There's something in this room."

But Frederick Van Tassel did not answer; he had seated himself for a long vigil, watching the Blind Spot.

XVI

FLANNING'S VENTURE

IT WAS A grim wait after that. The German, once the miracle had given its manifestation, had closed up like a clam, sitting quietly, while he waited, his eyes set on the place where the dot of blue had appeared on the ceiling.

Two hours went by, during which the nervous attorney explored the recesses of the house, going over the rooms upstairs and turning the books in the library. Finally he walked over to his Aunt Selena's, with a view towards lunch.

The old lady had prepared just what he was after. She set it out on a tray, and brought forth the inevitable apple pies. With this as an opener, he returned to the silent German, spread the meal on the table and called him over. Frederick Van Tassel ate

"You know," he said, when he was through, "I haf been having a lot of thought. Dot thing in there reminds me of a friend—a Professor Heisen in Berlin That was long, long ago. We were discussing a little thing called life Und Heisen told me a peculiar thing. He says: 'Van Tassel,' says he, 'mebbe we will never know what it is. But just the same we know it iss—don't we? Some day dis life vat you see, will be found—what you call, isolated. And ven we do dot—whuff—ve will know everything.'"

"Then you think it's life?" asked Fuillard.

"Mebbe it's death," came the grim reply. "But bah! Vat do we care about that? It iss good to die learning something. Und"—pointing with his thumb—"in there iss a secret of the Universe."

However, he did not return to his vigil; instead, he began

going over his notes, taking more, and peering through the odd corners of the building. But not for a moment was he idle; the day had drifted along; soon it would be dark. Flanning woke up, staggered into the library. The German asked for the papers he had found, went over them carefully, and asked for the detective's experience.

At last he spoke.

"There is no doubt of it at all," he announced. "We're in some sort of vibration—a sort of vestibule of the Unknown. It's governed by frequency—and ruled by time. But just what dot period may be, we cannot tell. Mebbe it's a minute. Mebbe a year—or a lifetime."

He pointed to the stone in the panel. "If you will notice how it acts. Put your hand close by. Radio-active—like der X-ray—only different. Everything—vibration. Light—matter —electricty—Life! Und if everything else answers the law, why must one thing be excluded? The Rhamda was a real scholar. He could have told all the scientists of the earth cards and spades. He could make matter. Ya! Und he could control it just so far—no father."

He smiled suddenly and nodded to the attorney.

"Vat does your aunt, der one who makes der pies, think about der business?"

"Ghosts!" came the answer.

The German laughed. "Und she's right, mine friend! She's right. All my life I live a skeptic; but now I know. It's ghosts w'at lives in the Blind Spot. Mebbe it's a little piece of hell, eh?"

His humor was sardonic; fatalistic. "Sure," he went on. "The good Doctor Holcomb, he says to his class how he will lift the screen of the Occult. He got killed. But I'll bet he learned something first." He consulted his watch. "Let's see. I've been here eight hours. Und I want to sit up all night. I think I'll take a little nap."

THE SPOT OF LIFE

Whatever could be said about Frederick Van Tassel, he could not be accused of an overstress of emotion. He was as cool as ice, deliberate. The atmosphere in the house was tense—void-like in its immensity. Yet he did not care. His short back disappeared through a bedroom door; five minutes later he was snoring.

"What do you think of him?" asked the attorney.

"I—I wish I had his nerve," answered the other. "I thought Hal Watson possessed courage; but that little fellow—"

"Just a matter of viewpoint," grunted Fuillard. "Lack of emotion. Mathematics! Cold as steel. It's a problem with Van Tassel—that's all. With us it is something else—mystery, life and death, a fine young man taken before our eyes. Calamity! What will happen? Also, I can feel the stress every minute—it gets on my nerves; I feel like I'm about to explode. I could not define it if I had to."

"What happened while I was asleep?"

Fuillard related the incident of the blue dot, and the sounds, especially that of the ringing bell.

The detective nodded.

"Exactly. That's the same thing that happened when the Spot took Hal. I didn't see the beginning, but I got the end. A flash of iridescence. He was knocked into kingdom come. Yet the little fellow is right when he calls it vibration. The stones govern it somehow. I'll swear to that. The trouble is—to set them off. It's like playing with dynamite."

"What do you mean?"

"Just this," answered Detective Sam Flanning. "I'm sick of waiting. And I don't propose to take this thing as a Dutch experiment. When I called you up, I had just been knocked cold. And—"

"You mean you wouldn't have called me otherwise?"

THE SPOT OF LIFE

"Not that. Please don't mistake me. What I'm getting at is that I want to reach Hal Watson. I was blurred and confused then; but now I've had some sleep—"

"Still I don't get you."

"Well, I'll come right out with it then. I'm going to shoot the works. And if there's such a thing as getting through, I'm going to take a dive. They got that kid—and I'll follow."

"How about your friend in there? It really wouldn't be fair to leave him out. And how will you go about it?"

The detective pointed towards the stairs. "Up there," he said, "is where we'll set it off. I don't know just how the thing works, but each time it has brought results. As for Van Tassel, mebbe he wouldn't stand for me making the experiment."

The snoring in the next room had suddenly ceased; the place became silent. Jimmy Fuillard opened the door and glanced in at the Blind Spot. But there was nothing unusual in sight. He turned back.

"Tell me," he whispered, "just what I am to do. Make it as definite as you can."

Detective Flanning did that; finally, when the last detail had been arranged, he took off his coat and rolled up his sleeves, announcing:

"This time I'll be ready. How's my automatic?" He patted his pockets. "Everything is all set."

It was a hard moment; looking the detective in the eye, Fuillard could feel that he would never see him again— and that death would be the sure result. He gripped the officer's hand. His lips moved:

"Flanning. You're a friend worth having. You—"

But the other cut him short.

"Shucks," he grunted. "This ain't nothin'. Like our German friend says: 'It's an honor to die learning something.' "

The other turned; a second later his steps sounded pit-apatting up the stairs. Detective Flanning looked in at the German, saw his body sprawled out, and backed away. He felt that he was getting his last look at the world. Softly he stole to the door and gazed down at the city; then with a nod he returned and opened the door of the Blind Spot.

Nothing happened. For five minutes he waited, peering for the beginning of the miracle. The silence deepened; there was only the weirdness of his own breathing and the pounding of his heart. Not that he was afraid—far from it. It was the suspense. Finally he stepped through the door into the library and listened at the stairs.

What was wrong?

"Hello," he called. "Hello! Fuillard!"

A sound of some one shuffling around was his only answer; the door at the head of the stairs creaked on its hinges, pounding out a volume of sound. Then, footsteps again. Some one whistled and dropped into a humming tune.

Yes, it was Fuillard. Perhaps he was just slow. Detective Sam Flanning returned to the library, stopped and waited, listening. All at once he heard a sound—a man was walking directly behind him. Came a voice:

"Vat iss?"

It was the German, armed with a heavy automatic, peering through his spectacles. The air was snapping with suppressed magnetism, electric, almost afire.

"Vat iss?" came the challenge. "Oh! You! I see. It was a dream I have—such a wonderful dream—and dot little—" then noticing Flanning in his shirt sleeves. "Where is Fuillard? Did something happen? Hey, Flanning! Listen!"

From the head of the stairs came a strange sizzling murmur—like the splash of red-hot iron in a bucket of water, streaming and seething, followed by a different sound behind them. They looked at the stone in the panel; it had

THE SPOT OF LIFE

suddenly reddened, turned into blue and dropped to a snow whiteness, alive and sparkling. Simultaneously a splash of clamor came from the room of the Blind Spot.

It was a bell—tolling, tolling! That everlasting tocsin, pounding its rhythm of clamorous warning.

"Ding dong! Ding dong! Ding dong!"

Flanning reached the room first, the German banged behind him. Both men hung back for an instant—listening. The bell continued; but there was not a thing in sight—merely the walls and the soiled paper on the ceiling. Behind them came a rush of steps—a man running down the stairs.

But Sam Flanning had no time for that—there was a sound behind the bell; it was increasing into a roar—a screaming and shouting. The roar grew to bedlam—increasing gradually in tone and volume like a mighty sea

There it came—the dot on the ceiling a livid blue—like all the hues of the rainbow centered into that one color, coruscating, flashing, afire, followed by the drooping string of incandescence weaving like a snake, pulsating and alive. It seemed to grow—filling the room, spreading.

There came the glimpse of vision—a vast throng, facing a round circle of white—a million beings in a storm-tossed landscape; or was it a building—vast, immeasurable, like the seething immensity of an ocean whipped by a typhoon. And every one of the million was gazing towards the room of the Blind Spot.

It was an army—a surging mass of uniformed men, moving towards the stairs and the round white stone. Three men were waiting in the center, while another stood to one side, frantically lifting a long bamboo up and down. The bell clanged again! One of the leaders rushed forward. At the same instant, Sam Flanning, the detective, leaped to meet him. Then—

There was just one split second of vision; the man with

the bamboo leveled his stick, the whole thing vanished, and Flanning toppled upon his face.

Van Tassel sprang for his friend. He was calling to Jimmy Fuillard.

"Quick! Quick!" he was saying. "He is dying! *Mein Gott!* It has come true! Now I haf seen der Blind Spot!"

XVII

INSIDE THE SPOT

THE HUMAN mind is a miraculous instrument.

The last thing that Hal Watson remembered was that streak of incandescence, the form of a man he knew as the Senestro, and Flanning. The whole scene had been jumbled into a conflict of rolling, fighting bodies. Then he had fallen into the light. After that he knew nothing. But now—

He straightened up, groped about, looked around. His mind was still in a whirl; he could not believe what his eyes were seeing. His ears caught strange sounds, indescribable and weird. Yet he was still Hal Watson, alive and alert.

That was the most important thing of all.

But where was he? What had happened? Certainly he was no longer in the house at 288 Chatterton. The very air had changed; there was a suggestion of immensity, a roar like a battling army. Then—like a flash, his surroundings began to visualize; he looked afar at a scene of bewildering proportion.

It was like no place on earth—a niche cut out of storms, cyclonic, a sort of throne with a sweep of silver stairs that dropped like the flow of leaping water. And beyond, as far as he could see, was an amphitheater, crowded with living beings, shouting, gesticulating, frenzied.

But what an amphitheater!

His eyes swept on towards the distance, where countless columns twisted themselves to the heavens, like inverted waterspouts. Architecture beyond conception—all of it woven into color, as tremendous as the crack of doomsday! It might have been a temple—anything. Hal Watson staggered back.

THE SPOT OF LIFE

The roar continued; strange bugles were sounding. The rhythmic vibration had given way to martial clamor. He could see an army marching, straight for the stairs. That was his first sensation.

The second was more relative. His feet began to tingle; his muscles twitched as though he had suddenly transgressed a field of magnetism. But it was not electricity, as he had known it. Rather, it was subtle, filling him with life and exhilaration. What could it be? What?

He glanced down, moved his foot, and wondered. He was standing on a peculiar substance, white as snow, circular in shape, and about twenty feet in diameter.

A snow stone! The same substance he had seen at the house at 288 Chatterton—magnetic and alive, built into a dais that extended about sixty feet on either side, hedged by silver walls, polished and adorned by golden scroll work. Behind him was a throne, cut from a solid jewel—green as the purest emerald.

It was like a dream—or a nightmare! The roar continued; he could hear drums and bugles. The silver stairs had filled with the oncoming bodies. Suddenly, a line of figures circled about the dais.

Figures? Men and others! The men were garbed in crimson and gold, splendid creatures; and handsome. But their companions.

Hal Watson gasped.

They were not men at all; rather, they were animals, gorillas, half human, half beast. Catlike, they circled about the dais and waited.

But Hal Watson was growing strong. He moved about, puzzled but unafraid. From his toes to the top of his head he could sense the power of the snow stone. He was a man inspired. He turned to the head of the stairs, where one of the red clad warriors confronted him.

99

THE SPOT OF LIFE

It was the Senestro!

The man was speaking; his lips curled into a sneer, his handsome face flecked with evil.

"Ha! Sir Watson," came his words, "I have you! At last you have been delivered to my hands. The secret of the Spot of Life shall be revealed. Kneel to the Bar Senestro!"

But Hal Watson had no such intention. He could not understand why; but each flick of a second doubled his strength. Kneeling was against his inherited instinct. His answer was a laugh. Again the man spoke:

"You would defy the Senestro? Fool that thou art. Know you not that you are destroyed—already dead? Fool! Today—tomorrow, in twenty-four hours we will conquer. You and your kind will go! I tell thee, kneel!"

This time he swung his arm. From the depths of the cyclonic temple arose a roar like thunder. Around the dais the Mongol-faced gorilla men crouched, their teeth bare, every muscle aquiver. They were setting on their toes ready to spring. Like a man in a dream, Hal saw it all—the line of figures about him; the red clad men on the stairs, and the Bar Senestro in front of him. Beyond, was the dim immensity of receding distance—a million men, clamoring for he knew not what.

It did not seem real. It could not be real!

"I tell thee, kneel!"

It was the Bar Senestro barking the command. But for some reason, Hal did not move.

He was galvanic, his muscles were tingling with the strange essence of super-vibration; his mind flashing with genius strokes. Whatever his life was to be, he was sure he would enjoy it. Still that command.

And simultaneously with the command a green light appeared in the distance—vast and round, like a living flame.

100

THE SPOT OF LIFE

It circled in a pinwheel, shedding concentric rings and finally dimming into a yellow dot.

Instantly the clamor changed. This time it was a yell of despair—screams of rage. The Senestro turned; he held something to his lips. A shrill whistle was the result. Instantly the line of gorillas charged. Hal Watson struck with rights and lefts; living the ecstasy of death. The dais swarmed with hairy bodies; they surged and twisted, heaving him up and on towards the stairs. And at last one of them must have struck him. The lights went out! The world was filled with darkness!

When Hal awoke he was in a different place—apparently a selected apartment; at first glimpse it looked like an anteroom, circular in shape and splendid in design. The walls were curved, circling from a domed ceiling almost to the floor, built of neither wood nor plaster; and colored with beautiful onyx. The effect was perfect; streaks of mixed and bursting hues, reds and greens and vermilions, shot with golds and silvers, polished with an easy, comfortable sheen.

The room might have been thirty feet across, with a doorway at either end; but with no sign of a window. A bench or two adorned the sides, with several rugs of an unknown texture upon the floor. Next, he noticed the bed upon which he was lying—a heavy posted Napoleonic affair with a canopy top. The coverlets were soft; the material was more than silken, and lighter than any stuff he had ever known. Straight in front of him was a sort of clock, half-way to the break in the wall, ticking the solemn music of time.

"Tick tock, tick tock."

That was the only thing that was natural. It reminded him of waking on a summer's day—with the sun shining, and the vigor of life calling him into the outside world. Yet—

And then his mind woke up. He straightened and stretched, gaped, and looked again. For the first time he really became conscious of what had happened. He remembered the gorillas—the Bar Senestro, and the temple of the storms. Once more the notion of dreams returned. The thing simply couldn't be possible.

He lay back on the pillows, gazing at the surroundings—scenting a perfumed air. From afar came a strange murmuring undertone, musical with the vibration of tiny bells—the same rhythm he had heard through the Blind Spot.

And that brought him back where he had started. The Blind Spot? Oh, yes! Everything was becoming clear. The whole drama paraded before him—from the beginning.

This was the Occult!

Professor Holcomb, his grandfather, had promised to tear away the screen that shrouds the unknown—to flood it with the light of day. But the professor had become lost. And then his own father had been killed. And there was a detective named Flanning who had come to Hal's home in Berkeley. He had told a strange story and they had journeyed over to the house at 288 Chatterton. There they had discovered the new stones and watched the phenomenon of the Blind Spot. Again the question came up:

Was this the Occult? The place was real, as certain in substance and material as the earth. And he was alive! Alive? The words of the Senestro rang in his ears: "You are dead! Given into my hands!"

Could it be true?

Hal Watson sat up in the bed; he pinched himself to see whether he was awake. There was no doubt of it. And yet— Something had happened. He felt sure that he was close to the room at 288 Chatterton. Perhaps he was in the

102

same apartment. And if that were so, the places were identical. He recalled a law of physics. "No two bodies can occupy the same place at the same time." The law is furdamental—as certain as the fact of substance.

He was stunned. The sequence of events whirled by, one after another, until he arrived on the snow stone. He recalled the gorillas, and the man who had ordered him to kneel. Then—the end had come!

But the most puzzling fact of all was that every scene had been consecutive down to the very end. It was like predestination, the working of some vast law. But what was the law?

Life or death? They are facts; and therefore have a law to govern them, a law, that, once known, would explain everything. The man who held it could rule destiny!

He lay still, listening; suddenly his attention was attracted by a shadow beyond the first doorway. He noticed that it led into a long corridor. Some one was moving, talking softly. He heard the voice:

"He's the one! The Bar Senestro will have it out of him before night. Then we shall see the day. What say you?"

But the man addressed did not reply. Hal Watson strained his ears, listening. What could the speaker mean? What was the information the Bar Senestro was after? And why the tone of suspense? Once again, he went over that last moment upon the snow stone—the scene in the temple, and the rush of murderous gorillas. Then, just as suddenly, he thought of the house at 288 Chatterton, of his own San Francisco, and his friend, Detective Flanning, all of them unaware of the danger.

Danger of what?

Could it be that the horde he had seen was planning to break through? It didn't seem possible; but if one could go,

103

so could a million. He listened again; but there was no further sound. Then he glanced to the side of the bed where his clothes were spread upon a wooden bench. In a moment he had slid from the coverlets and dressed. He started for the door.

But just as he reached the threshold, the shadow dropped across his path. A soldier in uniform stepped before him, saluted, and barred his way.

"Wait, my lord! In a moment!"

At the same time the soldier made a gesture with his hand and whistled. Immediately a number of unseen doors gave forth a guard, lining the corridor from end to end; soldiers, as erect and disciplined as any he had ever seen. Simultaneously an officer appeared from the far side with two of the unseemly gorillas at his back; saluted, and marched to their head. Hal noticed his military precision and pride; but he could not understand the beasts, shuffling along behind.

They were almost three feet wide at the shoulders, their arms dangling to their knees, their black eyes snapping viciously. Now and then they gave a chattering sound, looking this way and that. Six feet away the officer halted. Hal Watson spoke:

"Well," came his words, "you look good. And you seem natural. But first of all tell me what it's all about. Where am I?"

The officer answered in English:

"That, my lord, you will know presently. I shall take you to the royal Bar. The Bar Senestro! King of the Thomalia. Come!"

The guard wheeled, forming behind. The gorillas stood on either side, the officer in front. Hal Watson felt exactly like a man between two vicious dogs, expecting every second to be bitten. At the command he followed the officer.

104

THE SPOT OF LIFE

The company swung into step. But not so the gorillas; instead, they lurched along leisurely, snapping their teeth as they walked. Finally they came to the far end, passed through an arch and into a long room. Undoubtedly they were in some immense building.

At the end of the hall was another corridor opening upon some sort of a plaza and leading to a stairway wide enough for twenty men to descend abreast. All of it seemed to be constructed of onyx—carved and splendid. The air was perfect, perfumed by an unknown fragrance. From afar floated that undertone of melody he had noticed from the beginning. That and something else. As they approached the landing, Hal Watson caught the sound.

This time it was different; confused, tumultuous—the voice of a great city, of a multitude. He could hear traffic, shouts and clamor. And above it all, he could catch the indefinable exhilaration of suspense—the vibration of a mob. It sent a chill up his spine. The gorillas by his side turned to look, clicking their teeth and chattering. Ahead of them was an open door leading to a balcony far above the street. Hal looked and wondered.

It was a place he had never seen—a vast city, tremendous with domes of myriad colors, minarets and spires, streets and plazas; multitudes and sounds. The fact was tremendous—and beautiful. Again he caught that fragrance, and music; like all the flowers and birds of the world in the joy of June-time.

At first glance it might have been a convention; but almost immediately it became a vast throne room, magnificent, with silver walls and golden scrolls, the whole thing wrought by super craftsmanship into a setting as superb as the work of a Michael Angelo, and fused upon the central point of the building—two low thrones at the end, both of them carved from a substance which Watson

105

could not identify, but which might have been amethyst or sapphire. The thrones were casting a scintillating light—obscuring the occupants with a blaze of glory.

Hal Watson was blinded with the effect. But presently he could see. One thorne was occupied by a maiden—a princess in beauty and in fact. The other, slightly higher than the first, held the Bar Senestro!

XVIII

THE THREAT

It was Hal Watson's first chance to study the man, or rather king, for surely here was a royal setting. The Bar measured up to his rôle, as handsome as an Alexander, perfectly poised, his splendid body clothed in a dazzle of red and gold. But it was the same man with whom Hal Watson had battled only a few hours before—the man who had come only a few days previously for his father in Berkeley.

The king arose; instantly his handsome face altered; a sneer curled his mouth.

"Kneel!" came the command.

Hal could feel the guard filing around him, forming a crescent; the two gorillas stepped closer. But, for some reason, he had no intention of obeying. His eyes sought the princess on the lower throne, caught her glance and interpreted a soft curiosity. Her jeweled hand was half lifted; her lips parted.

"Kneel!" This time the king waved his hand; but he was stopped. The princess half rose; the kindly interest in her blue eyes had become something else. Her words snapped:

"My lord Senestro! Beware! Wouldst thou have thy equal kneel?"

"My equal?" The king had turned, his voice soft and scornful. "Doest thou call this weakling my equal?"

"Aye, my lord Senestro. Thy equal—perhaps thy superior. And as for the weakling—I can see by his eyes that he is a better man in the stuff that makes pure manhood. Remember, he is a prince of my own people. Aye, beware!"

THE SPOT OF LIFE

She had half risen, her breast heaving, her anger defiant. The creatures behind Hal's back chattered and snapped their teeth. The Senestro took a step forward, made a sign with his hand. Instantly the guard drew closer. One of the gorillas caught hold of Hal's arm, almost pinching it off. But immediately the queen rose. Her beauty became intense. She swung her hands.

"I tell thee, stop! Caswa! Balwa! Thy queen speaks. It is my pleasure! Thy master is before thee! Touch one hair of his head and I will slay thee on the snow stone. Caswa! Balwa!"

The effect was instantaneous; the two gorillas stepped in front of Hal Watson, chattered incoherently and knelt down. The queen spoke again.

"Sir Stranger, they are thy slaves. The only things in the Thomalia who can be thy friends. They and myself. The power of the Senestro shall not pass beyond the Spot. Let thy legs stand firm. Kneel thou not to a Senestro!"

Hal Watson could feel a multitude of eyes glued upon him. He looked at the king, expecting an answer; but instead, the Senestro broke out in laughter.

"Ah," he snapped. "Little vixen! Spoken like thy mother—the Nervina! Thou wouldst defy the Senestro even as she. But remember, her followers and thine are dwindled. She is no more. The Senestros are supreme. The Rhamdas are extinct. Your philosophy is dead. In its place we have truth. The laws of dimension—and facts! We shall 'solve the Spot of Life. And we have the man!"

The queen had returned to her throne; it was plain that she was helpless; she kept clasping and unclasping her hands; all the while looking at Hal Watson. Suddenly she rose again.

"Wouldst thou?" she asked the Senestro. "I know his people. They are brave and noble. Look thou at this man.

108

THE SPOT OF LIFE

Canst thou not see that he is handsome? Better than thyself."

The words were spoken out of the heart, helplessly. Hal Watson could sense the despair, without knowing the meaning. Nevertheless, it was easy to see that, down deep, was a great purpose. Who could the queen be, and what was her relation to his own kind? And who was the Nervina? A murmur arose from the multitude. From afar, beyond the building, came a deep boom, like a bursting of a rocket or bomb.

The Senestro listened; he spoke to one of his counselors; turned toward Watson.

"Thou art indeed handsome," he laughed sneeringly, "but helpless withal! Knowest thou the meaning of this?"

He waved his hand. Hal glanced at the assembly, at the array of soldiers and the senatorial dignitaries in front.

"I know nothing, O Senestro!" he answered. "I cannot understand. I return the question. Where am I?"

"Perhaps you are dead." The words came clearly. "Perhaps not. That is for you to find out. Knowest thou of the Occult?"

Hal Watson was staggered; once before he had been pronounced dead. Each step he had taken had seemed to confirm the promise of his grandfather. Yet for all that, he was still very much of the living. He glanced over at the queen. She was watching his every move.

"I know nothing," he answered. "It is like a dream. Only yesterday I was in Berkeley; and now?"

"Thou are in Thomalia," the other interrupted, "in the city of the Mahovisal! Behold!"

He gestured with his hand; one of the officers of the guard stepped forward, caught Hal by the arm, and led him to the window. Instantly, the world seemed to change, to open up its vastness and engulf him. He had caught a

109

glimpse once before; but what he now beheld was past believing.

The city was without end, extending along a vast plain, filled with plazas and parks, thronged by an army, tented, bivouacked, prepared. The landscape was full of serried columns, troops as far as he could see. Beyond lay the blue waters of a peaceful ocean, and over to one side, the sweep of a terrific mountain. He drew back. What was the meaning of the great army?

The Bar Senestro immediately sensed his thought.

"How long," he asked, "do you think San Francisco can stand against us? They go within twenty-four hours. And then you and thine—the human race—shall end."

The pronouncement was stunning. The earth man was silent; he could not believe. But not so the queen. She had risen, defiant to the last.

"Perhaps it is so, my lord Senestro," she said, "for well I know you would destroy my people. But remember! The secret is not thine. Your science has failed. And but for the—"

The Senestro laughed. "Aye," he answered, "and but for the cycle of the Spot of Life, we could not succeed. But remember! I have, myself, gone through. And here before me I have the man."

He clapped his hand; a group of soldiers stepped forward. But at the same instant the queen spoke:

"Caswa! Balwa! Do thy duty."

What happened Hal Watson never knew. The action was too swift. The huge gorillas had swung like cats, reached out for the soldiers. Men flew here and there. One of the guards was thrown through the air, splashing against the side wall. A whistle was blown. Immediately the fight stopped. The queen beckoned.

"So, my lord Senestro," she snapped, "beware! And remember, there are others! This man thou shalt respect. 'Tis

110

I that have spoken. The Aradna, daughter of the great Nervina, queen of the Thomalia. Defy me if you dare!"

And with that she turned from the throne, spoke to her maids in waiting, and was gone.

XIX

DISINTEGRATION

FLANNING WAS dead or very close to it, after that encounter with the Spot.

Van Tassel began lugging the detective's body into the library. He placed it upon the couch, ripped open the shirt. But there were no marks. Jimmy Fuillard was bathing the man's forehead. He asked:

"Dead? Van Tassel, tell me, is he dead?"

The other worked frantically; finally he looked up. His eyes had a strange look.

"Call a doctor," he said grimly, "quick. But be sure you get a physician with common sense. None of these quack know-it-alls."

Jimmy Fuillard needed no more; in a moment, he was at the telephone. Ten minutes later an automobile stopped at 288 Chatterton. A doctor of middle age, slightly bald, ascended the steps, turned about and looked around. Fuillard met him at the door, conducted him into the library. Van Tassel was leaning over the body.

"So," he muttered, gleaming at the doctor. "Here he is. Do what you can; but no monkey business."

It was a queer way to talk to a physician. Jimmy Fuillard wondered. The doctor knelt, went to work. Suddenly he looked up, began asking questions; but the German cut him short.

"Vat I want to know is whether he is dead? No, he ain't sick. Dot man wasn't sick a day in his life. He was perfectly well up to a half hour ago."

"I would call it a heart attack," replied the surprised

THE SPOT OF LIFE

doctor. "But I don't think he is dead. I'll summon an ambulance, take him to the hospital for treatment."

"Und kill him," cut in the German. "No. You won't do dot. If he's alive, he has a chance. But that chance comes right here in this house. The man is dying of vibration. *Ja!* We keep him here."

A physician runs into all sorts of amateurs; but here was a man who was different. The atmosphere and the setting were unusual. He looked over at Van Tassel.

"Vibration?" he asked in a puzzled tone.

"*Ja!*" said the German. "You do not understand. Neither do I. But it iss so. Vibration and dimensions. Here he will live. Out there," pointing to the door, "he will die—like a fish out of water."

The doctor drew Jimmy Fuillard aside. At the mention of the Blind Spot, he lifted his eyebrows. Apparently he had read the story in the newspapers. He glanced in at the German who had crossed the room and was fumbling by the desk.

"Let me see," he said. "Professor Watson died of a heart attack, didn't he? This Blind Spot? Say—" He stopped and listened. "What's in this house?"

"It isn't natural," came the answer. "Wait a minute. I'll try to explain it to you."

Jimmy Fuillard explained what he could; then he conducted the doctor to the door and allowed him to walk through the veil of silence. The other listened, looked at his watch. Plainly he was puzzled.

"Let me see," he spoke decisively. "I have a date at the hospital. I'll call my colleague. This thing is too interesting to leave—also too important. Besides, there is that patient inside."

Jimmy Fuillard took him over to his Aunt Selena's. A moment's work at the telephone was sufficient. Dr. Colyer was ready for the Blind Spot, anxious to uncover the phenomenon that had overcome the detective. First of all they moved the unfortunate Flanning to a bed. The doctor nodded to Van Tassel.

"All right," he said softly, "now I'll take a look at that room."

But the German shook his head; he pointed to the bed.

"How about that man Flanning?" he asked. "I asked you once—is he dead?"

"No."

"All right. Dot's all I want to know."

Without a word Frederick Van Tassel turned back to the desk, dug into the drawers and came up with a box of paper. He grasped a pencil and began dashing off figures. Jimmy Fuillard was astonished at his friend's rapidity—equations were born, formulas leaped out. The man had become an automaton, impersonal, scarcely alive. The doctor opened the door of the Blind Spot, peering inside. But of course, there was nothing.

Nothing?

Yes, there was, too. A flicker of sound drew his attention. Or was it sound? Jimmy Fuillard was looking over his shoulder. Suddenly he, too, caught the scraping, inarticulate movement. He stepped inside. At first he could see nothing; but presently he located the disturbance.

It was on the back wall, the one next to the kitchen, a tiny speck no larger than a pea, where a perfect hole had been eaten, or burned, straight through the partition, for all the world as though it had been sprinkled by some powerful acid. Yet there were no fumes and none of the ordinary reactions of a chemical nature. Even as they looked, the sides of the tiny aperture dropped off, disappeared.

The phenomenon was undoubtedly atomistic — beyond chemical explanation. The doctor grasped the fact at once.

114

Here was matter disappearing into space. He turned about, beckoned to Van Tassel. Whereupon the pudgy German dropped his pencil, entered the room, stood with his hands clasped behind him.

"Well," he asked brusquely, "what about it?"

It was too much for Dr. Colyer.

He gasped. Here was a miracle being worked before his eyes, and yet—the pudgy German was taking it as a matter of course.

"Can't you see?" he exclaimed. "That wall is being eaten up. It is disintegrating. It isn't natural."

But the German only nodded. "That's only w'at you think, Dr. Colyer. There isn't anything that ever happened in this Universe dot isn't natural. Otherwise there wouldn't be any Universe. Iss it not so?"

The doctor nodded; but Jimmy Fuillard was skeptical, exasperated.

"All right," the attorney snapped, "then you explain it. Explain this cursed Blind Spot—the whole damned mystery."

And that was just what Frederick Van Tassel proceeded to attempt.

XX

THE INFINITE

It was a tense moment. First of all, the squat German conducted them into the library, waved them to chairs. He removed his spectacles, put on another pair.

"Fuillard," he said tersely, "I can't say much. We haven't the time. Every minute counts—every second. If we solve this thing, we must work together. Do what I say, and don't ask questions. As soon as I've told you what I know of this, I want you to hurry down to my apartment. Here is the key. Bring back that little green trunk in the corner of my study. Also the top drawer in the heavy files.

"Get back here the instant you can. And—" speaking to the physician, "doctor, you better stay here. Our patient may need you at any moment, and, and—something may happen to myself. Even before I can tell you my theory of the Blind Spot I may be struck down—snatched away.

"So," he flared. "Mebbe you think I am fooling. Eh, Fuillard? But I am not. I tell you, it may mean disintegration —the end of the world! I should not be wasting this time now—but if something should happen to me, others must have my knowledge to carry on the fight.

"Now—you have read the paper of Professor Holcomb, Mr. Fuillard? I mean the scrap where he announced his lecture on the Blind Spot. What did he say?"

"He was going to solve death—and lift the riddle of the Occult," answered the attorney.

"Did he do it?"

"How do I know?" answered the puzzled Fuillard. "At least he did something. He was caught in his own discovery. But solving Death is some task."

116

THE SPOT OF LIFE

Van Tassel turned abruptly to the doctor.

"Did you ever study physics? Mathematics?"

"I'm a doctor," came the nervous answer. "The only physics I know is of a medical nature. In high school, yes—enough to understand a few principles such as the law of Archimedes and several others. Mathematics? Well, just what was in the curriculum. No more."

"I see."

Van Tassel turned, swooped behind the desk and came up with a collapsible blackboard, straightened it out and picked up a piece of chalk. He glanced at the attorney.

"Pardon me," he spoke brusquely, "if I go into big figures. But that is right where we start from, here in the Blind Spot. Now watch, and see what I do.

"For a starter I am going to give you the beginning of the answer in absolute numbers." He turned about. First of all he wrote:

$$H = .000000000000000000000655$$
$$\text{erg-sec.}$$

Whereupon he glanced at his companions. Both men gasped; it seemed that the procession of ciphers would never stop. The German's eyes had become bright; he beckoned with his chalk.

"You don't understand, eh? Well, after all it isn't your fault. We can't know everything. This is the last equation of higher mathematics; the farthest that the human mind has been able to go. It is known as the second law of thermodynamics. But even that is all Greek to you. Is it not so?"

There was no doubt of it; both men waited impatiently, fidgeting. The doctor glanced apprehensively toward the Spot room. The German went on.

THE SPOT OF LIFE

"Perhaps I should put it in another way so it will be more intelligible. For instance, this second law of thermo-dynamics is merely the mathematical calculation of the end of the material universe and its energy; when the sun, the moon, the stars—every atom of substance shall have given up its treasure of force and become nothingness. Do you get me?"

Again there was no answer; again he continued:

"No, you don't—quite. Why? Because it is an abstract concreteness, worked out in errorless sequence, down to the very end. As mathematics it cannot be shaken; nevertheless, its very perfection is puzzling. For example, you and I know that energy is passing out of matter at a tremendous rate; the world is growing cold; the sun is dying; and some day the last moment will be at hand. Yet, we do not consider the problem in a serious light. But how about the mathematician?"

He waved his piece of chalk; underlined the figures.

"Here is their answer. It is the end of their higher mathematics; the place where they must stop. That equation tells the story. Wherever the student of advanced physics gathers for his discussion, he is confronted with this second law of dynamics. It is met everywhere; all the atoms of all the elements will be destroyed when they lose their energy; the process is going on in every corner of the universe. Only—"

He stopped; the piece of chalk snapped harshly in his fingers.

"It cannot be. That law is a delusion. Every physicist in the world feels it; but he can't prove it. Why? Because mathematics is a perfect science; figures do not lie. So something must be radically wrong. What is it?"

He pointed tensely to the room of the Blind Spot; his eyes brightened behind his spectacles.

"Your Professor Holcomb had the answer. He found the

118

secret; but he was caught. In the Blind Spot! Ah! There we have it! But let us go back to mathematics; for, as I say, they never lie.

"However, after all, figures have a way of going around the corner and sitting down. And that's exactly where we are at the present moment."

He paused, wiped his face with his handkerchief.

"I have only a little time to explain. Others who have guessed at this secret have vanished before they could inform the world. I must speak fast. But I wish to assure you that we have a few facts to go on. There is a chance that we can solve the Blind Spot. However, the danger is great. That little pinpoint on the wall is merely a beginning. Disintegration! Ja! It will spread over the world. The deluge is at hand—unless we stop it. So! But wait! I was speaking about Professor Holcomb. He started out to solve death, which, after all, is merely another name for life. Do you understand what I am driving at?"

Of course they did not.

"Here's what I mean. The second law of thermo-dynamics is the final computation of mathematics—an equation that equals the Universe run down, all its energy consumed, converted into nothing. Absolute zero!"

He paused for a moment; looked down at his auditors. Then he continued.

"But right there is where sophistry leads us out. We know that nothing can go nowhere; if a thing goes at all, it must have a destination. Otherwise, we would have chaos instead of Cosmos. We merely fool ourselves. It is like saying that when we turn the sack inside out, we lose the hole.

"What is life? No man knows." He turned to the blackboard, still talking. "Life is here all about us; we know that

119

it exists. Then, suddenly, it disappears. It is gone. Gone where?"

He touched the scalloped fringe on the outside of the circle, turned about. "Can't you see what I am driving at? Our whole Universe must answer to one law; and the same thing that governs the energy of the atom, governs life."

Doctor Colyer nodded; suddenly he spoke up.

"I think I get your point. You are speaking in terms of dimensions. Nothing is ever destroyed; so it must go somewhere."

"Exactly," said Van Tassel. "It's a tremendous problem when we compute the life of a material atom which will not give up all its energy for uncounted trillions of years; but when we look over the miracle of life, it is different. We see the thing every day. We have this second law of thermo-dynamics working before our eyes. Life is real, else it wouldn't exist. It came from somewhere; and somewhere it must go. You understand now. Ah—"

He paused dramatically, pointed to the next room; his words were ominous:

"There we have the answer. Some one has harnessed the second law of thermo-dynamics: $H = .0000000000000000000000000655$ erg-sec. The next chapter in human destiny! Surely it is the greatest day since Columbus. It proves what I have been working at for the past twenty years, namely; that mathematics does not stop with the second law of thermo-dynamics; instead of that, it merely begins. And when we get into the real facts, we discover that there is no end, that we live in a perfect circle. This Blind Spot will go down in history."

"But what is it?" asked the attorney.

"That's for us to find out," answered the bespectacled Van Tassel. "I can only tell you that some one far greater than ourselves has been working. He was mightier than all our intellects put together; compared to him, Newton, Laplace, Descartes, Einstein, combined would be as a baby. A super genius of a higher plane! *Ja!*

"He must have solved the law of dimension; he built the Blind Spot. To do it, he must have held the secrets of the coefficients of matter and of spirit. It is the point of contact. Right here where we are standing is the miracle of lost energy and death. We must thank Professor Holcomb for what we know. But we must be careful lest we meet a like fate."

"How about Hal Watson?"

"We don't know yet," came the reply. "But Hal Watson went through alive. I have hopes."

"How about these coefficients of matter and spirit?" asked Doctor Colyer. "What are they?"

Once again Van Tassel raised his hand; it was a gesture of impatience. He pointed to the circle.

"You have not studied the higher physics, the new mathematics of the future, or you would not ask. For instance, we have several—length, breadth, thickness, time, motion, energy, space, inertia, stress and consciousness."

He paused at the last word, adjusted his glasses, and looked into the room of the Blind Spot. Finally he turned around.

"*Ja!*" he repeated. "Consciousness! Perhaps it is the greatest thing of all. We do not know. But mathematics has a way of going ahead of experiment. Take Einstein, for instance. He proved his relativity with figures. After they had told him that he was crazy, they went along with their experiments and found that he was right. But what he discovered is only the beginning. How little we know!"

Again he held up the stick of chalk; this time he snipped off a piece about a quarter of an inch long.

"For instance," he said, "in this tiny speck of white

121

substance there are a hundred billion billion atoms; each one a tiny world—for all we know—a Universe! Ions and protons; suns and stars; each revolving at an inconceivable speed about its separate center. All answering the same fundamental order! Underneath is a common force—we call it electricity for convenience—governed by infinite coordination. Remember! From the most infinitesimal ion to the farthest star, we find harmony. Nothing happens except through law!"

Van Tassel was through. He turned to the desk, flopped into a chair; he reached out for a mass of calculations. But suddenly he looked up again, barked at Fuillard:

"But you must go, quickly!"

XXI

THE SECRET

THE SITUATION was grim. Fuillard put on his hat, stepped to the door. Outside he commandeered the physician's car. In a moment he was speeding down through the city to Turk Street. Before he was aware, he had stopped in front of the wholesale jeweler's.

The same slim individual rose to greet him, but at the sight of Jimmy Fuillard's face the jeweler's jaw dropped.

"Where's Fred?" he asked. "Hello! What's happened? You look about twenty years older. Say, listen—"

But Jimmy had not time; he stated his errand. The tall one led the way upstairs. As they entered the room the fellow turned about, his gaunt features a picture of curiosity.

"Here you are," he said. "So he wants the green trunk, eh? Do you know what's in it?"

"He didn't say. He told me to get it—and not delay. That's all I know. And then there is something else. Oh, yes—that top drawer in the files. Now then."

"Did Fred do any figuring? Tell me—"

"Some. Why?"

The other was holding the rear of the trunk, descending the stairs; at the bottom flight he stopped and glanced in the store.

"Because," he said, "if he did, I'm going with you. As you know, Fred Van Tassel is the top mathematician of all the earth. He's positively uncanny."

Fuillard returned for the file; when he came down the stairs the tall man was waiting. "You fellows are getting all the kick," he announced, "so I'm going to headquarters to get in on the fun."

But when Fuillard explained what had occurred, he was not so jovial. Still, he had a word or two of encouragement.

"Leave it to Van Tassel," he said. "If it can be proven by figures, he's the baby. Did he tell you anything about his theory of dynamics?"

"As much as he had time for."

"I see. Well, that's his hobby. A graduate of the University of Berlin; chemist for a living, and a mathematician for sport. I've known him for twenty years, and he's never stopped figuring. It's his only pleasure; where you and I would go to the theater or a ball game, he pulls out a sheaf of paper and starts in. Funny thing—he says that Einstein has stopped at the beginning. That the realm of mathematics is merely in its inception."

"Perhaps he's right."

Fuillard was thinking of the last few hours. Things had happened so rapidly that he was ready for anything.

Just then they turned into Chatterton Place, stopped in front of the dwelling. The jeweler sniffed the air, looked up and down the street. Then without another word he began helping with the trunk. The German was waiting in the hallway; he fairly ran to assist them. A minute later he had jerked the cover open and was running his hands into a sheaf of papers. Finally he picked one out and spread it on the table.

It was covered with radical signs and tremendous fractions, arranged in the formula-like precision of cryptic calculation. For a moment he was in deep study. Then he seized a paper and started out on a new set. Dr. Colyer had stepped from the bedroom; he motioned the others inside.

"What's in the trunk?" he asked.

"Figures."

"I thought so. And I guess we'll need them. They say mathematics is the perfect science. Well, let's hope it is.

THE SPOT OF LIFE

Van Tassel hasn't spoken a word since you left. He's been hopping around with that tape. You'd think he was an architect. There he goes now!"

They looked through the door. The stubby German had finished a row of figures and banged the last with a pencil. Immediately he started for one of the back rooms. For a moment he was gone. Then he returned. His voice rang out.

"Hey! Come here quick!"

Three volunteers stepped forward. But the first one was his long-legged friend, Couland. Without a word Van Tassel tossed him the end of the steel tape, bade him hold it in the center of the mysterious room. Then he took a grip on the other end and began measuring the distance to the stone in the library, standing on a chair and lifting the tape. Something happened, though just what it was, no one could make out. There came a faint sound—like a bird puttering through the bush. The German looked back. The jeweler was holding his end near the center of the other room. Van Tassel spoke.

"Are you ready?"

"All set, Fred."

Once again the German lifted the tape, holding the leather case in his hand. Simultaneously a streak of fire ran along the floor—a poisonous green—unholy in its hue—like a flash of lightning. The tape was gone—had disappeared. The jeweler leaped through the door.

"Holy mackerel!" he exclaimed. "What was that?"

But Van Tassel had scarcely moved; a cold calm smile played about the corner of his lips, he nodded.

"That, my friend," he spoke in answer to the question, 'was some of our dynamics. Dynamics with a move on! You see, it didn't take the atoms in that steel tape a trillion years to lose their energy. Not by a long shot! They went all at once. Yust like a man dying. That's discovery number

125

one. Here is the other." He pointed to the library stone. "We have found the coefficient of acceleration. Now we can work."

Where did Van Tassel get all his inspiration? The jeweler knew better than the rest; he nodded his appreciation. Certainly the tape had vanished; and just as certainly the white jewel in the library panel had something to do with it. The easiest way out was to lay the blame upon some mysterious aspect of electricity. But Van Tassel would have none of it.

"No," he answered, "it is not that. It would take me hours to explain. But we are on the right track, which is enough. You see that wall inside the room? It is breaking to pieces. Soon it will be doing more than that. This whole building will go. And then—"

He had returned to the desk, caught up the papers, and resumed his figures; suddenly, however, he turned to Fuillard.

"I'll leave the explaining to you," he spoke. "Take the gentlemen upstairs and show them the other stone. But don't touch it. Under pain of death leave everything as it is. We must do nothing until I have solved some more phenomena."

Fuillard did just that. The doctor and the jeweler peered within the sacred precinct, examined the ice covered stone. The jeweler was the most interested of the three. He could not get away from the thing. He shook his head.

"I've heard of this house years ago," he said, "and I remember the story about the other stone. It was lighter than air!"

"And a solid?" asked the doctor.

"Exactly. But we didn't believe it, of course. Yet—the man who told the story was a reputable chemist. But that, as I say, was years ago."

"What do you think about Van Tassel's theory of dynamics?" asked the doctor. "According to his idea, everything is possible—even our dreams."

Fuillard did not answer; he was thinking of that vision through the Blind Spot—the hordes of human beings, the great white stone and the men standing beside it. But now that he thought back, there was, somehow, the element of illusion. Perhaps after all, it was some supervillainy. Things just simply had to fit in with his idea of dimension. Still—

Just then he turned and looked around. For some reason both the doctor and the jeweler had left the room and were gazing through the door across the hallway. Immediately the old sensation came back, pregnant with silence and that everlasting isolation. The jeweler was drawing a long breath, looking around. From below, a chair scraped along the floor. A voice floated up. Came the words:

"He was going to solve death; but he found something greater. Professor Holcomb! His son-in-law, Professor Watson, and last of all Hal Watson! A whole family!"

Was Van Tassel talking to himself? The voice sounded far away, as though it were coming from a deep well. Also, there was a sense of loose dimension, wherein the ordinary circumstance of a man's balance suddenly became shifted. In a way, it was like a man falling. But almost immediately the sensation disappeared. Again the room was silent. Fuillard looked at his companions. Both were pale as death.

"What was that?"

It was the doctor who spoke. The jeweler caught the wall with his hand. He called out:

"Van Tassel! Oh, Fred!"

There was a sound from below. The German appeared at the foot of the stairs.

"What do you want?"

"Were you talking?"

"No."

THE SPOT OF LIFE

"Then come up here and listen."

The chemist climbed the stairs; heard their story. The four men stood still; but this time there was no sound but the beating of their own hearts. The doctor shook his head.

"Beats me," he muttered. "I've heard about this house; and now I believe. There's somebody in this room occupying this very air. I'd swear I'm going to believe in ghosts."

His words were gruesome and hollow; but apparently they meant nothing to the analytical Van Tassel; already the little fellow was plugging back down the stairs. His voice held the same cold judgment.

"You'll believe in a whole lot more before we're through. Ghosts? Bah. A ghost is a figment of the imagaination. What you are going to see will be real. Your little legend of death will be a dream. But stay right where you are. Don't move until I return."

It was easier said than done. There was not a coward among them; but there are times when any man will favor the open air of daylight. The attorney spoke up as Van Tassel did not come back."

"What do you suppose he's doing?" he asked.

"Most likely he's gone back to his mathematics," said the jeweler. "Anyway, he didn't seem to be excited. If I had his nerve I could do anything. I bet, doctor, you're wishing you had kept your date at the hospital."

It was a lame attempt at humor and it died on the speaker's lips. Once again there came that vague suggestion of sound—rising from the bowels of the earth. It was like an earthquake rolling over—or the hum of a thousand powerful motors.

Haroom! Haroom! Haroom!

And because it held a certain mechanical purr, all three men immediately began associating it with some past experience. Perhaps, after all, there was something that could be explained. But just as suddenly the sound changed, lilting into a cadence that floated along the air with a musical rhythm. There was no direction; unless it came from their feet. As the sound died down, the attorney called again to Van Tassel.

"*Ja!*" came the answer. "I heard it. Now listen again. Now!"

This time the sound was nearer—a confused babel of voices, indistinct, lifting into a roar; then stopping.

Dr. Colyer glanced at Jimmy Fuillard. His words were cryptic.

"It's Van Tassel," he said. "What has he got? Those sounds weren't in this building. Listen."

Once again they heard the thing—like the pattering of hailstones upon a slate roof, striking with a terrific impact and fleeting away into the distance. A light shone at the foot of the stairs, white, and then bluish, forming a ball like Saint Elmo's fire; a man was standing behind. Not until he had reached the top step did they know it was Van Tassel.

"Well," said the German softly, "you heard something, didn't you? *Ja!* And so did I. Now we'll see what else."

In his hand he was holding the box-panel containing the library stone, moving it about like a search light. Sometimes it was blue; then it would be white. But always he was careful to keep the rays off his companions, shifting it up and down along the walls; finally he turned.

"Strange," he muttered, "I thought I had it. Perhaps, after all, this is not the stone I took it for. We better go downstairs. You first, gentlemen."

Once again he returned to the desk, allowing the others to shift for themselves. The doctor glanced at the detective; the jeweler walked to the outside door, and Jimmy Fuillard peered into the room of the Blind Spot. Van Tassel kept working, plodding and now and then using a compass under a diagram. Finally he was satisfied; he motioned to the doctor.

"See, this is what I have found. Here is the Blind Spot." He pointed to a round hole in the center. "And here," indicating a circle, "is the first stage—a concentric ring of influence about twenty feet from the hot spot. Do you understand?"

The doctor did not answer; the German went on.

"Of course you don't; but I've got to tell you. See? First a dot und then a ring. Remember that. Then out here is another ring—which really reaches to the opposite side of Chatterton Place—concentric impulses working from a common center. That is very important also."

He placed his pencil upon the dot representing the Blind Spot and drew a straight line to the outer circumference, cutting it at a spot represented by a figure, reapeating the performance in the opposite direction. Again and again he drew the line; until the whole was cut into a ten-pointed star with traverse lines and intersections. Finally he rose in triumph. "There," he declared, "is your Blind Spot. Right here in this building—with a little lapping over on the outside. Perhaps I am a little wrong; but the principle is there."

The physician marveled; he turned the paper around.

"And you figured this all out by mathematics?" he asked. "You did it in a few hours?"

But the German was not open to compliments; he snorted; his hand went up in a gesture of impatience.

"Hours!" he exclaimed. "*Mein Gott,* doctor! I have been working for thirty years, figuring day and night. But I had nothing to go on—just the calculations beyond the last law. I was laughed at for a fool. But now"—he waved his hand proudly—"here iss the proof—the very point of contact—

the space beyond the end. We have found it. Perhaps the thing will kill us; but what of it? We will die happy. Iss it not so? I may never see another day. But—" He passed the diagram on to the doctor. "You keep the paper. Remember, it is the map of the whole thing. If I die, be sure and summon the scientists. Take the stone and let them see for themselves. You know enough to explain."

XXII

FROM THE VOID

JIMMY FUILLARD had suddenly returned from the room of the Blind Spot. For a moment he, too, studied the paper, glancing first at one man, then the other. His face was ashen, his eyes set. For a moment he did not speak. Then:

"A map, eh?" he asked. "Everything down. But—" He pointed into the room. "Before you go any farther, why not look at the spot on the wall? Your disintegration has run up against a snag. Come here."

There was no doubting his actions. Fuillard had seen something; he was stunned. In another instant all three were inside the apartment. Fuillard was pointing to the rear wall, where the disintegration was peeling off the molecules. A hole about ten inches had been eaten out—revealing the kitchen beyond; also something else.

At first it looked like a green light—a mystic lantern hung by an invisible thread, giving forth a blinking, unholy glow; but almost immediately it materialized into fact and substance. It was a stone—as large as an egg and as green as an emerald. No jewel could compare with its beauty; no talisman equal its significance.

For it was alive, potent, and portending. Its light was not like that of the others; instead it flashed and cooled; sometimes it diminished into a mere pinpoint; again it would enlarge and cast a greenish color about the surroundings. Strangest of all, it was suspended in pure air, apparently independent of the law of gravity. Van Tassel gave an exclamation; rushed forward.

132

THE SPOT OF LIFE

"What is it?" asked Fuillard. "It's there all by itself. And what are those flashes?"

The chemist had caught up a chair, sat down; for several moments he was as silent as the proverbial clam. Fuillard was at his right, the doctor upon his left. The physician still held the diagram in his hand. One and all, they looked and wondered. Finally Van Tassel reached over for the paper, spread it upon his lap and caught up his pencil. Half abstractedly he marked a dot within the inner circle. Then he turned his attention to the intermittent flashes coming from the stone.

"What is it?" asked Fuillard.

The answer was silence; Van Tassel held up his hand. But it was plain that he had made some sort of a discovery. He had drawn his chair closer; his eyes glued to the stone. The flashes appeared in regular order, like so many words repeated over and over. Ten minutes went by, a half hour, without the German saying a word. Finally:

"*Mein Gott!*" he exclaimed. "It cannot be. It cannot be."

Jimmy Fuillard was dying with impatience; he caught the chemist's arm. "For Lord's sake," he begged, "tell us! What has happened? Explain!"

Van Tassel moved his hand; looked at the stone and spoke:

"Get me a piece of paper. Quick! Several blank sheets out of a box, and a pencil. It's—it's Doctor Holcomb—the great professor of the Blind Spot, alive and talking.!"

The thing had gone beyond believing; Fuillard fairly stumbled in his haste; in a moment he had secured the required material, was thrusting it into the hand of Van Tassel. The doctor crowded closer, watching to see what he could gather from the lights. But only Van Tassel could make them out. First of all he began writing.

"This is Doctor Holcomb. This is Doctor Holcomb. This is

133

THE SPOT OF LIFE

Doctor Holcomb. Flanning, Flanning, Detective Flanning. S O S, S O S, S O S!"

The light stopped, went out completely. From a far corner of the building there came a faint undercurrent, rippling— like the semblance of a whisper. The three men listened; but the murmur had died even as it rose. Immediately the light began sputtering again; for all the world as though the power was running out. The German breathed a prayer:

"*Gott* give us time! Dot **s o s** means plenty of trouble. And Doctor Holcomb is alive. But where is he? If I could only answer—get a word across."

The stone seemed dormant for the moment; first it was a poisonous green, then a healthy emerald hue. Sometimes it reminded of death; then again, it promised life. Van Tassel mumbled his thoughts:

"It's vibration," he said grimly, "yust like I said when I first came into the house. There should be a number of stones—this and several others. But there isn't any doubt about those signals.

"They're in code—that **s o s** is as plain as day. He knows that there is some one here. He thinks it is Flanning. Hello! There it is again."

This time the flashes were faster; the chemist contented himself with dots and dashes, which the other two could not understand. For a full five minutes the signals continued. Van Tassel was straining every nerve; beads of sweat rose from his forehead. Once he breathed:

"*Mein Gott!*"

As the light went out again, the same rustle of breeze sounded behind them. But it did not distract Van Tassel. He was looking over his paper. His lips moved; his hand trembled. Suddenly he turned to Fuillard.

"It's worse than we thought," he spoke. "We have only twenty-four hours. And then—"

THE SPOT OF LIFE

"Then what?"

"It will be the end. At least as far as the human race is concerned. The professor," pointing to the stone, "is sending the message through. He keeps calling for Samuel Flanning. Flanning, Flanning, Flanning. Here it is all over the paper. And down below is this:

" 'Hal Watson is safe. He is alive!' "

"Can't you see?" said the German. "They are two against a billion. There the light goes on again! He's calling for Flanning."

The sequence continued for two minutes, almost despairing in its repetition, finally dying into a cryptic sentence which the German wrote down carefully, word for word.

"I shall keep this up as long as I can. Let God by my guide, and lead some one to the other side!"

Van Tassel looked up; the three men were dazed; it was too much like a spiritual seance—impossible. Yet they did not doubt. Something had to be done. Dr. Colyer nodded.

"We've got to signal through," he said. "The old professor will be talking in the dark until we flash our answer. Wait a minute!"

He reached up with his finger and touched the stone. Immediately a strange thing happened; the color turned to a milky white, then vanished. Simultaneously the physician turned to his companions, his face a study of emotion.

"Humph!" he mumbled half aloud. "I never— Say, touch that thing yourself. Did you ever feel anything like it?"

But the stone had disappeared; in its place was only a tiny pinpoint of light, scarcely visible, receding before their eyes like a distant star. The German gazed at the doctor.

"What happened when you touched it?" he asked. "Tell me."

135

THE SPOT OF LIFE

Dr. Colyer shook his head. "I don't know. I couldn't explain it in a dozen years. You'll have to feel it yourself. Exhilaration! Ecstasy! Like life!"

"That's vibration," said the German sharply. "You did a foolish thing when you touched it. It could have killed you just as easily. But it is something to know. Hello! Here comes the light again. Wonder where it has been? Ah!"

This time it was like a shooting star, a meteor of mystery cutting though the heavens, all in a few seconds, finally focusing in the center of the hole. It blazed for an instant; then it began a series of dots and dashes. The German seized his paper and pencil. Suddenly he looked up—his eyes shining, every muscle set. His voice choked.

"Doctor. Doctor," he spoke to the physician. "We have got it. You have sent the message through. Listen to the answer."

This time he translated the dots and dashes.

"Who is talking?" came the words. "Is this Flanning? This is Professor Holcomb. Do you get me? Did you receive my s o s? If so, answer. But do not touch the green jewel with your flesh. It will set up a vibration; it is not of the earth. Touch no stone inside of the Blind Spot Room. There are two others. Go to the library and take the white jewel from the panel. Perfect insulation. Send Morse code."

The German was elated; he stood up. But before he could move Fuillard beat him to it, caught the white jewel from the panel and dashed back. In a moment Van Tassel was ready, holding it against the green vibration. At first he was puzzled. How would he work it? But just then he drew back; again the light had deepened, spotting its intensity in a series of apparent signals. The chemist followed the dots and dashes with his pencil. When the light stopped, he translated:

"Professor Holcomb speaking. Take the white stone. Don't

ɔe afraid. The two vibrations neutralize. Use the white jewel ıs key."

That was all. The men leaned forward; the German held t up, lifted it toward the green light, tapped softly and re-ɔeated. What he sent through, neither of his companicns cnew; but it brought results. Once again the stone almost disappeared, for all the world as though it were carrying the nessage in person. Finally, there came a faint flicker. It ɡained intensity, glowed like a burning coal. The German wrote with his pencil—in code. Finally he looked up.

"Ja!" he spoke enigmatically. "It's what I said in der first place—vibration. Spot of contact; over there," indicating the ɔenter of the Blind Spot room. "Just what I have already proven with the steel tape. Beyond the end is the beginning."

"But Professor Holcomb? Where is he? What does he say?"

"He is alive and Hal Watson is with him. Says he's in Thomalia—wherever that is. Mebbe it's heaven—mebbe it's hell. And he thinks I'm Flanning. Wait a minute and I'll try again."

This time he telegraphed quite a message, albeit he was rather slow. The two men could gather the substance from inference. At last the German drew back and waited. This time several moments elapsed before the light came back.

"It isn't possible," Colyer declared. "Too much like talking to spirits. Do you suppose he's dead? It can't be."

But once again the calm little German shook his head.

"That's only because you are human," he answered, "and have built up your structure. Death? Bah! It is only a dream —a bugaboo to frighten babies—and men. You will see. You say that you cannot understand; but that, doctor, is merely because you are five-sensed and accustomed to a three dimensional experience. *Ja.* Three dimensions and five senses. Dot is all you know. But your Einstein has proven that even gravity is relative and that time and distance are forever

137

on the move. In other words, he has opened the door for a new conception. Man stands on the threshold of a new destiny. Hello! Here comes the light."

The thing seemed to leap out of the distance, like a mystic headlight. It glowed, became larger, and materialized into the stone. This time it went to work with a vengeance. Van Tassel seized his pencil: five minutes went by—ten; and still the chemist worked on. But at length he stopped. He turned around; his usually calm face was as white as milk.

"Six hours. Ten! Mebbe twenty-four," he said, "and then—the end of the world! But we have word from Professor Holcomb." He pointed to the hole in the wall where the atoms were dropping off into space. "He did that to attract our attention. It was a desperate chance, because once started, only one thing can stop it. Fortunately we are in the house of the Blind Spot. The professor calls it the Spot of Life. And we were ready. *Ja.* "Gentlemen," he waved his hand. "I cannot explain. I can only ask you to obey. A few short hours. There is so much to do. And I alone can perform the miracle. You—"

It was one of those minutes when Fate writes the decision. Both the older men had risen. They were calm, set, ready; and they did not ask questions. Van Tassel nodded, picked up the white stone and walked to the room where Flanning lay upon the bed. He glanced up at the doctor.

"Now," he said, "I shall prove to you that I was right when I told you to leave him in the house. Heart disease? *Ja.* But with a vibrational origin. This is what I learned yust now from Professor Holcomb. Watch!"

He stooped over, took the white jewel in his hand and pressed against the stricken man's head. For a moment! Then—the man stirred, a foot jerked under the coverlet; a flicker of intelligence passed over the features and the eyes opened. Flanning sat up in the bed, looked around.

138

THE SPOT OF LIFE

"Who—who?" he asked. "Where am I? What was it? Oh, I see. But—"

Plainly he was stupefied, half conscious; his mind was far away. He kept gazing into space.

"What is it?" asked the doctor.

The detective passed his hand over his forehead as if endeavoring to recall a picture.

"I don't know," he answered softly. "I might have died —I was a billion miles away. Listen! There it is again."

It was the same rustle they had heard several times before, soft as a zephyr, accompanied by that weird motion of shifting dimension. The walls of the room faded. The electric light dimmed. The detective had drawn himself to the edge of the bed, straightened up.

Then—there was something else.

At first it looked like a mist or part of the shadow; but almost immediately it materialized into a human form.

Human? Hardly! Rather, it was a gorilla, massive, featured like a Mongol. A great uncouth creature standing in the center of the apartment! It turned about, gazed this way and that—its black, shoe-button eyes snapping viciously; until suddenly it located the detective. Whereupon it reached under its arm and brought out a creese. The thing flashed in an arc, straight for the detective's heart. A cry of horror went up. The three men leaped—too late.

Bang!

It was a healthy pistol shot, coming from the door, one that hit the mark. The gorilla-like form staggered backward, clutching its arm; disappeared. Simultaneously a mistlike shadow drifted across the room, illusive and suggestive. Then— the light became vivid again, revealing the human faces— especially that of Detective Sam Flanning and another in the doorway—Couland, the jeweler. Came his words:

139

THE SPOT OF LIFE

"I got that fellow! But who was he?"

The detective had risen, testing out his feet. His eyes were uncertain—querulous. He looked around, first here and there. Then:

"That's the one!" he exclaimed. "He was here—in the room. I could see him in my dream."

The German was standing still; his face had not altered. He nodded.

"*Ja*," he said, "you thought it was a dream. I know. But Fred Van Tassel is here to say it vasn't. Dimensions? I vas right. More than one. It's a good thing, Couland, you come in with the gun. *Ja!* Now we know. Mebbe you will believe me when I tell you we must hurry. I told you six hours. Mebbe it's only dot many minutes. Now listen—all of you."

He reached for a paper and began scratching names, passing them on to the doctor and Jimmy Fuillard. His words were crisp.

"Get these men on the telephone. Bring them here to this house. Right now! Don't take no for an answer!"

His decision was military, absolute. The men obeyed without question. The German turned to the detective, spoke again.

"Your memory by this time has gone?" he asked. "It was like a dream—except that last part. Vell, you have seen enough. I have something for you."

Flanning stepped forward. "What is it—you want the police?"

"Exactly," came the answer. "Get the chief right now. A riot squad. Machine guns! Gas bombs! All the killing weapons you can scrape up. And remember— Speed! This will be worse than war! The old Battle of Thermopylae was fought on a mountain. This will be fought in a house."

The detective fairly leaped; but just as he was going through the door the German called out. The officer stopped.

140

THE SPOT OF LIFE

"What is it?" he asked.

"For Lord's sake, get me a telegrapher," called Van Tassel. "Get him here the instant you can."

XXIII

THE INDICTMENT

HAL WATSON, alone in a land of mystery, had found a friend. His mind blurred with gratitude and wonder, as the Aradna balked the hostility of the Bar Senestro. Was she the wife of the Bar? And if not—what was her relation? The Aradna? Doubtless a title. But the Nervina—who was she? And what was meant by the cycle of the Spot of Life?

The answer to that flashed as soon as suggested. Undoubtedly it was some phase of the phenomenon he had come to know as the Blind Spot. And what did the Senestro mean by the term "dimension"? Who were the dignitaries in the scarlet robes? And the Rhamdas? Finally, what had his father to do with these people?

A murmur rose from the assembly. Once again a rocket boomed out in the city, followed by three others in quick succession.

The effect was startling. There was a rush for the windows, but the guard drove them back. The Senestro stopped, listened; then he turned about and gazed up at the wall behind the throne. A great red circle had suddenly materialized. Hal noticed a green light flashing in the center, winking, and going out. Finally it blinked again. Another rocket sounded from afar.

The assembly had come to an awed silence, faces white, expectant. The Senestro had not stirred. From the recess of the tremendous building a bell was pealing, booming its solemn notes. The king held up his hand, counted.

"One, two, three! That is all!"

The green light in the red circle faded out. In its place

142

was a many faced dial with a number of hands working toward a single point. The Senestro pointed; turned to the assembly.

"See," he spoke. "The moment approaches. The calculation is perfect. I promised to bring you proof; and I have this man. Through him we shall solve the Spot of Life. When that dial reaches the zero hour, we shall have come to the end. But the end will be the beginning. The greatness of the future is before you."

He clapped his hands; guards caught Hal by the arm, conducted him to a door. The two gorillas followed, chattering.

Hal Watson found himself in a sort of library, lined with books and furnished with tables. Over to one side was a long blackboard filled with figures. Some of the symbols were in hieroglyphics, but part were in English. One thing struck him in particular—a tremendous decimal at the head of the board. It read: $H = .00000000000000000000000000665$ E.S.

Below were a number of formulas and a jumble of calculations winding up with a symbolic $X = .0$.

The guard had stepped to a far door. The two gorillas were waiting, imperturbable, one on either side. Hal Watson went over to one of the tables, picked up a book. To his surprise it proved to be an English classic—none other than the fifth volume of Gibbon's "Decline and Fall of The Roman Empire." Beside it was an atlas—one of the very latest editions, containing marked maps, and tables. Glancing over at the wall he picked out a shelf filled with geographic magazines.

It was beyond belief!

From the beginning he had believed himself in another world. But now? His conjectures stopped at the thought. Here were books, hundreds of them—in English! The fact suddenly dawned—everybody he had met had addressed

143

him in his own tongue, albeit they employed a rather sophisticated idiom. That idiom might have come from grammer. He had met foreigners like that. Yet—their accent was good.

He continued his research; titles began to pop out. He encountered some of the greatest names in science. Laplace, Volta, Faraday, Copernicus, Galileo. Then there were others —Newton, Pasteur, Leonardo da Vinci, together with a smattering of the philosophers. Text books abounded. Data, statistics, even baseball scores.

Where had they come from?

Finally he came to a desk with a number of papers scattered about. One of them, held down by a jeweled weight, attracted his attention. The writing was in a clear legible hand. He read:

Summing up, we find the following.

Their greatest mind so far is a man named Albert Einstein, a mathematical genius who might be remotely compared with our own Jarados, albeit he has only touched on the fringe of certain common laws, the first of which, called the theory of relativity, is the mere beginning of real thought. However, we find that there are very few who can understand him, and that the great mass of population is densely ignorant.

They have not reached down to the law of the atom; although they have discovered that it exists; neither have they any knowledge of ethereal structure. Their knowledge of dimension is limited to a superstitious reverence for death. They are cowardly, holding it a mark of distinction to risk their lives. This weakness threads their history, their economics, their philosophy, even their daily routine. They are ruthless, selfish, untruth-

144

ful. While making the greatest protestations of friendship, they will ruin their competitors in business. Always inconsistent; they are not so far removed from the ancestral baboon. Their history abounds in wars.

They do not appear to have any great knowledge of economics; hence we encounter the strange phenomenon of whole nations producing foodstuffs in such huge quantities that they literally starve to death! Each man strives to pile up as much as possible to ward off starvation; but unfortunately as soon as he has gained wealth, he becomes a marked man, with every other individual, through friendship, treachery, insinuation, violence or lust plotting to rob him. What is true of citizens is true of nations and peoples. From the first recorded event, we encounter great migrations, whole races sweeping across continents, slaughtering and killing. Murder is an art; deceit a virtue.

Yet, strange to relate, their loudest protestations, in government, business and in personal relations are just the opposite. They talk eternally of peace and a peculiar code of ethics which they call—love! They are entirely without honor. They merit destruction.

They ought to be easy. They possess no knowledge of atomic law; they are totally ignorant of the vast resources of light; and they doubt the existence of an ether. However, they have entered upon a chemical age, and are just skimming around the edges of its vastness. Quite appropriately they have turned most of their knowledge in the direction of destruction—explosives, gases, and poisons—with a view to more killing and greed.

Finally, they have no inkling of dimensional equation. However, a few of their minds—the aforementioned Einstein and several others—have dug down into

THE SPOT OF LIFE

the physical aspects of Universal Law and have reached as far as what they call the mysterious quantity H. Beyond that they have been unable to go. In other words, they have not solved life.

That was all; the remainder was set down in hieroglyphics, figures of unknown character with now and then what looked like the Greek letter Theta cropping out. But it meant a whole lot to Hal Watson. He read the wording over and over, inwardly acknowledging the indictment, at the same time resenting its implication. His own race—his own people had been found wanting. It was a sentence of death!

He glanced up. The two gorillas had not moved; yet all the while they were watching. Once again he looked at the blackboard where the cryptic formulas drifted down from the mysterious equation of H. He began to understand—to realize that he was looking at the vastness of the infinite, where Time and Space had become animate. He was not dreaming. It was a fact. Perhaps, as Professor Holcomb had prophesied—it was Death!

He stepped again to the window, glanced out at the vast city. This time he understood the scene. The army, the throngs, the unending columns meant—invasion.

The landscape was unending, beautiful. Out of an azure sky what looked like a swarm of swallows was dropping into the sea, casting up jewels of flashing spray. Airships! Each one as big as an ocean liner. Beyond was a mountain, Himalayan in magnificance, rising miles above the snow line. Over to his left was the sun, a dozen times larger than his own, standing on the horizon like a plate of mellow gold.

Hal Watson was fascinated; but suddenly he noticed the columns moving. At the same instant something stirred behind him. He turned and encountered the Bar Senestro!

146

XXIV

FATALISM!

THE KING had closed the door. He beckoned Hal Watson toward a chair, chose one for himself. His action was far different from the haughty demeanor of a few minutes previous. Yet he was every inch a despot—his words snapped arrogance.

"So you have seen?" he began, indicating the window. "What do you think?"

"I do not know," came the truthful answer. "I cannot understand. You have an army. Yet, this is not San Francisco. It is not my world. It—I cannot begin to understand."

The other nodded.

"Of course not. But you will in a few hours. When they begin parading down Market Street through a death-swept city, you will wish that you had stopped them."

"I?"

"Exactly. You and one other. There was your father; but he no longer counts. Tell me—who was with you in the house at 288 Chatterton?"

Dimly Hal Watson realized that it was to be a game of wits, with all the odds on the side of the Senestro. Should he answer him truthfully? The king awaited, his splendid eyes watching his victim.

"Who was with you?" he repeated.

"Flanning." Hal Watson let out the truth, scarcely knowing why he spoke; at the same time conscious of the other's magnetism.

"You mean the detective—the man who followed me from Berkeley?"

"Yes."

"What happened before that? Tell me, did the news-papers—your reporters—suspect the power of the Spot of Life—I mean the Blind Spot?"

"No, I don't think so. They accepted it as an old woman's tale."

The Senestro smiled. "And they didn't suspect the death of your father?"

Hal Watson started; instinctively he sensed the truth; his heart skipped a beat.

"What do you mean by that?" he asked.

The Senestro did not bat an eye; his answer was brazen, ruthless.

"Merely this," he answered. "I killed him, of course. I suppose they called it heart disease?"

He had pulled a small tube from his pocket—an object about the size of a flash light. He held it in the palm of his hand. Hal Watson was fighting down a thousand impulses; the strongest of which was to seize this calm villain and throttle him to death. His own father murdered!

The Senestro smiled; he stepped closer.

"I know how you feel," he said, "but it had to be. Your father knew the secret of the Blind Spot—part of it. And he had to go. I was also after you. But I did not have the time. I was forced to return. How did you pick up the case?"

Hal had gathered himself together; he was thinking of Sam Flanning on the other side of the Spot—a lone man bucking mysterious forces with a supply of bravery and pure ignorance. Yet a certain something warned Hal that he held a card. Otherwise the Senestro would not have sought him.

"It was just simply—well, the detective followed you.

148

He could not gain a hearing at headquarters, so he came to me. I accompanied him to Chatterton Place."

"How long ago was that?"

"I don't know—that depends on the time I have been here."

"How long were you in the house at 288 Chatterton?"

"About twelve hours—maybe a little more."

"And you picked up certain phenomena? Tell me how you managed to open the Blind Spot. Answer me that."

He turned the silver tube over in his hand; behind him the two gorillas were standing motionless, their black eyes snapping.

Hal Watson wondered what the object could be.

"I don't know how it opened," he said. "It just happened. Don't ask me why."

"I'll tell you right now," came the reply, "that you're a pretty good liar. Like all the earth folk, you fall back on deceit. No, no! Don't get excited. It will do you no good. Do you suppose"—he waved his hand—"that I would have you here otherwise?"

"And you killed my father?" The words boiled out. "And now I must tell you the truth—betray my friends?"

"Have your choice." The Senestro turned, stepped to the door, beckoned. A member of the guard marched in, saluted. Again the Bar turned to Watson. "Here is how I killed your father. Watch and you shall see death—as it should be."

The soldier had not moved; he was standing at attention. The Senestro adjusted a button on the small tube. Then he turned it towards the soldier.

"This man is not afraid to die—because he knows. Now watch. I have timed his end. Two minutes. Count the seconds. Ah. Now then."

Hal was horrified—fascinated; the whole procedure was

149

beyond belief. There was no feeling—no emotion. The soldier had not moved a muscle; a minute passed by—thirty more seconds; two minutes. The man fell down on his face. Dead! The Senestro grunted.

"There's your father's end. The way he died. Dimension! Do you understand?"

Hal Watson did not; he could not speak. The Senestro stepped to the door again, called another soldier. The scene was repeated, only—

"This time I'm going to drop the minutes," said the Bar. "I shall show you how a dimension gun works. Instantaneous—noiseless. Watch!"

It was done! The clean-cut soldier had met death without a whimper. His body collapsed. Immediately the guards outside the door marched in, gathered up the bodies and disappeared. The Senestro nodded.

"Perhaps you will talk now. Oh, I know how you fear death."

Hal Watson laughed. His fingers were itching for the other's throat. But greater than all was the menace of the Blind Spot. His own people! He had seen the dimensional gun. The vision of a death-swept San Francisco might become a reality.

"Perhaps I should show you something else. Come." The Senestro rose.

He led the way along a corridor—through a hall lined with silent soldiers and out on a portico. He pointed, far below, at the vastness of a temple, where an uncounted host was waiting. The sight struck the earth man like a blast. It was the same place he had seen from the mysterious snow stone; but viewed from the height it was titanic.

The Senestro stepped closer.

"Behold your Blind Spot," he said. "Behold the Spot of

150

THE SPOT OF LIFE

Life! Yonder is the secret. The point of contact. Our answer to your death. The end and the beginning! Mark ye well."

The words were dramatic. But Hal Watson was watching the pool of magnetism. It seemed alive, twisting, seething with an unholy glow. Soldiers were pacing around the edge; a blue-coated column thronged the silver stairs. The golden walls behind the throne pulsed, reflected glory. And far above, directly behind, was a green jewel. It gave off a winking light.

A roar sprang from the multitude. It swept through the storm-tossed temple and was caught up outside.

Suddenly the whole scene visualized. The earth man gasped. The Spot of Life had disappeared. In its place was the dingy room of the Blind Spot. A man was standing in the center of a faded Oriental rug. It was Flanning! Hal Watson leaped to his feet, let out a yell. But it was drowned by the multitude. The scene had vanished. The Spot of Life had returned to color.

Here was a proof of the unknown dimension. From the inside looking out! And he had seen Sam Flanning.

Something touched his side. He had forgotten the Senestro. But now—the handsome Bar was holding the dimensional gun close; he gritted:

"Now then. You're going to tell me. What's going on in the House of the Blind Spot! One minute! Then you die!"

151

XXV

A TRUMP CARD

It was a grim threat. Yet the earth man was not afraid. It proved one thing. The Senestro did not know it all. There was still a chance—if he only knew how to use it. Perhaps he could flash word to Flanning. Warn him!

And there was one thing more—the mysterious stones he had found on the other side. They were keys—undoubtedly. He faced the Senestro calmly. The Bar drew back; his face white with rage. The words snapped.

"You're a strange man—like your father, Chick Watson. But come. I still have a way. I shall show you."

Once again the earth man was led to the room. The Senestro pointed to the figures—drawing the calculation down to the final answer.

"If you won't talk gracefully, perhaps I can make you. Do you know what this is?"

Hal Watson shook his head. He was thinking about the scene in the temple—of the natural transition. In front of his eyes was the great decimal, signifying the mysterious quantity H. What manner of mortals were these people of the Blind Spot? What was the law? And finally why had his father remained silent? The Senestro spoke again:

"Did your father ever speak of the Thomalia?—Of the Spot of Life?"

"Never."

"Did he ever mention a man named Harry Wendell, or one Hobart Fenton?"

"He did not."

"I see. And I know you speak the truth," he indicated the

152

ooks upon the wall, and the paper on the table. "You
ave looked at these and wondered where they came from.
suppose you have guessed that much?"

"From Chatterton Place?"

"Exactly. Purloined years ago. They have been our source
of information. They have given us your language.

"We have learned a great deal about your world. We
now you; but you are ignorant of us. Only four men
rom the earth have ever gained entrance through the
Spot."

"Who were they?"

"First of all, there was a Professor Holcomb—a man who
might be compared to our Jarados. Second, Chick Watson,
your father, followed by one Harry Wendell and another
named Hobart Fenton. The last two became Kings of the
Thomalia. Your father returned to the earth and held his
secret. The professor—"

He stopped. Hal Watson spoke up.

"What became of Professor Holcomb?"

"We shall come to that later," said the Bar, looking
around. "I'm going to prove to your satisfaction that you
have no chance to escape." He pointed again to the decimal. "You will find that you are up against natural law,
that we know each detail, and are prepared."

He reached for a chair, sat down. Hal Watson wondered;
the Bar was one minute a king but the next instant he
could be a man. Certainly, he was an actor.

"This is the Thomalia," he declared. "A world. Round
like your own—and dimensional. In the beginning we came
out of chaos, I suppose, and passed through geologic ages
just like any other. But that was billions of years ago. Then
came life—and living beings. Men! And history. After that
we must have passed through epochs much like your own.
We grew out of savages, into what we chose to call civiliza-

153

tion. We produced men and events; and finally we had our Jarados."

"Jarados?" echoed Watson. "That is the one you compared with Professor Holcomb."

"Right. Because, like your grandfather, he was a scientist with imagination—a man far ahead of his age. To be exact, he was born in the Chemical epoch of the Thomalia. A great genius—something on the order of your contemporary Einstein, only far greater. The man who solved the atom, and built up the elements. How many elements have you on the earth?"

"Ninety-two," came the quick answer. "One or two are still undiscovered; but that is the correct number."

"Did it ever occur to you that there might be more?"

"Our scientists say there can be no others. I haven't given it much thought."

"Ha! Yet you know that all your elements are common at the bottom, built out of vibration, or what you choose to call electricity. For instance—your hydrogen atom is composed of two ions and a nucleus; whereas your oxygen is made up of six ions and a nucleus."

"Yes, that runs on up the scale—clean up to uranium."

"And you know that you can take two poisons—say sodium and chloride and produce a substance that is a food—salt. In other words, an exact opposite."

"I understand that much. It is one of the marvels of nature."

"Exactly. Well then, what do you suppose you get when you master the under laws of vibration and build up your own elements? For instance, why has your three dimensional world stopped at the ninety-second?"

The earth man could not answer; the other went on.

"Simply because it is the end of that dimension. Beyond, you step into something else. You find the door of another

world. Once opened, it solves the Infinite. For instance"—
he pointed—"The Spot of Life! Our Jarados, the great mind
of the Thomalia! The man who built up the laws, but could
not use them.

"The reason?" he went on. "Simply because he was born
before his time. He lived fifty thousand years ago—in an
almost legendary age, when the Thomalians were but a few
millenniums out of savagery. He could not pass on his
knowledge; no one could understand him. Hence he did
what any other genius would do under the circumstances.
He wrote down his laws, selected a few followers and taught
them what he could. His death marks the calendar of the
Thomalia."

"What happened then?" asked Hal Watson.

"Just exactly what always happens," came the answer.
"His followers regarded him as a god. They called themselves Rhamdas. And they built up a religion—one that sur-
vived for many thousands of years, a religion of the Spot
of Life and its prophecy. They promised the return of the
Jarados and his teaching. The Spot of Life would open.
And strange to say, it did."

"You are talking now of Professor Holcomb?"

"Precisely. The Spot of Life does run in cycles—the Jarados saw to that; no doubt as an inducement to the Thomalians. It was something to solve—they could not use it until
they had evolved up to its level. And then—when the
cycle came around, one of their Rhamdas, a head man,
passed through. And your Professor Holcomb stepped into
Thomalia. The Rhamdas hailed him as the Jarados. Later,
he was followed by your father, known as Chick Watson.
That was in the days of my own father—the first Bar
Senestro."

The Bar continued: "Let me go back a ways. I said there

155

was a religion with the Rhamdas acting as high priests. I failed to tell you about the Senestros—the secular kings who opposed them. The two orders had grown side by side. The Rhamdas taught science from a religious and supernatural standpoint. The Senestros held the opposite view—that the Jarados was a mere man, long since dead, and that there is naught in the universe but plain natural law. From the start, we have despised hocus-pocus. The people were divided.

"So naturally, when a stranger came through the Spot, it looked bad for us. There were two queens who had gone through. And there was a prophecy written on one of the golden scrolls. Everything seemed to dovetail with the sacred word.

"First came Professor Holcomb—a great mind and a scientist. Then came your father, answering still more of the prophecy. Then the first queen—we called her the Nervina, returned with a man in her arms. And then another man. Strange to say, each detail appeared to tally. The people of the Thomalia were aroused. The day had been promised when the Thomalians were to enter paradise.

"The Senestros were helpless. But they did not give up. From the start they had despised the Rhamdas. The whole thing was recognized as Rhamdic trickery. We knew that your men are mortal—poor earthlings of another world.

"That was known as the day of the Jarados. You might compare it with your own Day of Judgment. Millions and millions gathered, prepared to enter the Occult. There was only one thing the Senestros could do. That was to be ready, head the hosts, and lead them into the other dimension.

"But there was one man who beat us. Professor Holcomb! He alone understood the peril. He managed to get your father back to the house at 288 Chatterton. His mind seemed to equal that of the Jarados. And he did not relish the fact that he was acting the part of an imposter. His sole purpose was to save the earth. He succeeded; yet he failed in his ultimate intention.

"The day arrived. The very minute! The Trickery of the Rhamdas was supreme. The Senestros sought to lead the Thomalians—marched up the silver throne. The Spot of Life became a living thing. And the miracle happened— just so far.

"The Spot opened enough to convince the Thomalians. The Judgment of the Jarados became a glorious fact. The two men Harry Wendell and Hobart Fenton married the queens. They became monarchs of the Thomalia, and Professor Holcomb was forced to go on with his rôle of deceit— he became the Jarados.

"The Senestros were disgraced. For a while they were out of it entirely. But as I say, they did not give up. They still maintained the naturalness of the seeming miracle. They pronounced the Jarados an impostor. In the end, we formed our great conspiracy and succeeded.

"There was only one way—to destroy the Rhamdas, kill them one and all. It was a holocaust worth seeing. The two kings, known on earth as Harry Wendell and Hobart Fenton, were executed with their consorts. The only one left was the daughter of Queen Nervina. We call her the Aradna."

"And you say the Rhamdas were all killed?"

"All except one," came the blunt reply. "The Rhamda Avec. We could not reach him because he had been caught in your own world by the closing of the Spot of Life. But he must have learned. He and your father recognized the danger from the Senestros. They kept the Spot closed."

Hal Watson breathed a sigh of relief. At last he could understand his father's silence, also the reason for the own-

157

ership of the house at 288 Chatterton Place. The Senestro
continued:

"Since that day we have been working. Most of the
Rhamdic secrets became our own; we weeded out the
dogma and selected the facts. Every detail had been gone
into. And now we have come to the end. The dimension
has been solved. The way is open."

There was on thing left. Hal Watson asked:

"But why did you come to Berkeley? Why were you
looking for me?"

The Senestro looked up; his whole demeanor suddenly
altered; an expression of foxlike cruelty flashed across his
face.

"That is for you to find out," he snapped. "I killed your
father. He knew too much. I had to be sure. Two men
were in my way. I got one in Berkeley. The Rhamda
Avec I finished later. However, certain things have happened during the last few hours. Some one has been tampering
with the Spot from the other side. You are going to tell
me."

Again the earth man was silent. He was thinking of the
stones and their miraculous substance. Undoubtedly they
had been built up by the Rhamda Avec. The coming of
the Senestro had destroyed the plan. What did the Bar
refer to? Had Flanning gone for help?

"You are going to speak?"

"No!"

The Senestro snapped to his feet; his whole bearing had
become tigerish. Hal Watson glanced over at the two immovable gorillas in the corner. Their expression had suddenly altered. The Bar stepped to the side wall, pressed a
button. He sneered back at his prisoner.

"I'm going to show you something," he spoke. "You fear
death! Remember, I know the psychology of the earth

158

man. He is a coward; if not for himself, at least for others. You shall see."

Once again steps sounded along the corridor, measured, and even. The door opened. Two guards appeared. They were packing an object between them—a withered shape that bore the resemblance of a human figure, wrinkled, twisted, scarcely recognizable. Yet it was a man!

A man! Hal Watson staggered back. Two wonderful eyes were peering up—gray pools of wisdom, beautiful, calm, unafraid. The soldiers had yanked the form to its feet, jerked it about to face the Senestro. It staggered, fell against the side wall. The lips moved.

And the Bar Senestro laughed. He waved his hand.

"So," he taunted. "You that fear death! Look ye well into the future. Behold! 'Tis he. The false Jarados. Professor Holcomb!"

XXVI

THE ARADNA STRIKES

It was a blow to Hal Watson. What manner of torture could have reduced a human form to such a level? Professor Holcomb! The name had become legend. A thing to conjure with! And now—

Here was a fumbling wreck with only the eyes to tell of the spirit. They sought Hal Watson; peaceful, undaunted, unconquerable. The Senestro snarled. He had become fiendish. He arose to his extreme height, waved his lordly hand.

"Behold the Jarados!" he taunted. "The last remnant- of Rhamdic superstition! We salute you!"

Hal Watson was ready to strike. His anger was akin to frenzy; but something restrained him. He gazed at the aged form, caught a glance from the eyes. It was like looking into a soul. They were speaking more than words—they appealed. Here was intelligence supreme!

The Senestro sensed it. The earth man could study the flitting uncertainty of the Bar's handsome features. Something had gone wrong. What could it be?

The old man had gathered himself together. A bony hand reached up for his throat, caught the garment together, and dropped down. The lips moved:

"The Lord Bar is ready! Let him beware!"

Simultaneously a tiny bell tinkled at the end of the room, bringing a faint answer from afar. Hal Watson looked over at the two gorillas. He noticed the Senestro reaching for his breast. Suddenly the Bar straightened. The haughtiness returned.

160

THE SPOT OF LIFE

"Well done, thou Jarados!" he spoke. "But remember the end is nigh. We know the secret of the Law. See? We have brought thee a boon. Is he not a handsome specimen?"

The words were wicked, taunting. Hal Watson did not know their meaning yet he could sense the inference. Death was not far away. Outside, the guards were drawn up. A murmur sounded in the distance. Once again the bell tinkled. The Senestro turned.

"Thinkest thou to play with the Senestro?" he demanded. "Neither thyself nor the queen can stop me. 'Tis written in destiny. Thy fate is sealed. Unless—"

"So be it. My lord has spoken. If he holds the secret, why should he ask? Look ye well to what ye do."

Professor Holcomb looked down the hall, past the gorillas and back to Hal Watson. Again that warning. This time it was caught by the Senestro. The Bar stepped forward, seized the old man by the wrist.

"Fear ye not death?" he spoke. "Look at this man—Hal Watson. Thy grandson! What say ye now?"

Hal Watson clenched his fist. But once more he was stopped by the glance from the aged man. The Senestro turned about, touched a button. Immediately several men clad in long crimson robes appeared through a door in the side wall. But at sight of the aged form they stopped, reverence written in their features. One of them spoke:

"What now, O Bar Senestro? This—"

"Aye," came the answer. "Did I not promise that we would carry through on the day? Behold—the Jarados!"

He laughed. An orderly darted in from the corridor At the end of the room the many-faced clock ticked its solemn warning. The Senestro glanced at the message, wrote an answer. The guard disappeared. But as the door swung behind him, Hal Watson caught the roar of that tremendous multitude. The thing was getting on his nerves.

161

THE SPOT OF LIFE

Suddenly the bell tinkled again; this time there was a note of defiance. Simultaneously, the portion of the wall beneath the clock broke into a pale blue light, revealing a mirror. And in the glass a feminine figure! The Senestro had drawn back aghast. It was the queen—the Aradna! Came the words:

"Beware ye, Senestro! The day is come! But the Aradna has not spoken."

Plainly her arrival was unexpected. She stepped forth—a vision of blond loveliness, silken, her left arm bare to the shoulder—every inch a maiden—and a queen. She spoke to the earth man.

"I have watched ye from the beginning. Speak not! Thy life may be forfeit. The earth? My people—one word and it will be too late."

What could she mean? Hal Watson was dazed. The Senestro was clutching his weapon. The two gorillas stirred uneasily. Plainly there was something in the air. The little queen pointed.

" 'Tis so, Senestro! I know thy power. But remember I am the Aradna. Thinkest thou that I have no secrets of my own? I, the Aradna, daughter of the Nervina, and the godchild of the Jarados!"

She was defiant, her tiny foot stamping. Beauty supreme! And impotent! The Senestro tossed his head, broke into laughter. He pointed derisively at the frail figure of Professor Holcomb. But just as he moved his lips a sound drifted from the temple—mysterious, like an ocean rolling over in its sleep.

Haroom, haroom, haroom!

An earthquake might have equalled the effect—the building trembled and settled. The air deadened. Hal Watson was stunned. Then—the atmosphere changed. The lights went out. From the distance floated the sound of the tremendous bell.

Something swept upon Hal. He could hear the staccato command of the Senestro; a mighty arm caught him up and lifted him towards the ceiling. A cry! A roar! Quick words—commands. A light passed before his eyes, revealing the rushing body of the princess, heading for a doorway. Behind was one of the gorillas holding the professor against his breast.

Doors slammed! Curses! Shouts and defiance. Then all was changed. There came the sensation of rushing waters and swift movement along a silver lined passage murky with creamy light. They were going down, swinging around corners, and reversing. But suddenly they stopped. Once again the lights went on. The little queen was standing in front, poised and listening. The roar of the multitude was close at hand. It crescended like an augmented wave. But now it had a note of terror. Again the building shook. The girl had turned to the professor.

"Father," she asked, "what is it? Are we too late? What?"

Hal Watson witnessed another miracle. The bundle of wreckage suddenly straightened—became erect. Here was genius—superintelligence. Jarados or not, he was no longer a mere man. His words came softly.

"'Tis nothing my child. The earth is speaking."

They were standing in a circular room, with walls of glistening ebony, lit by an unseen ray. The effect was somber and threatening. But the queen and the professor knew their business. A flicker of color appeared before them, twisting in a spiral and focusing into a figure of three colors —red, green, and blue. A clover leaf! The princess toyed with the top color. She spoke to the earth man.

"Remember! You will follow. Turn neither to right nor left. The gorillas will protect you. Be not afraid. And re-

163

member, come what may, the Thomalians still hold respect for their queen. And the Jarados? He is supposed to be dead."

She had pressed the third color!

Immediately all things had changed. A blaze of light shone down from above. They were moving swiftly, gliding out upon a white substance—the snow stone!

Below was the multitude, waiting, terror stricken, uncertain. The faces were numberless, upturned, whitened. Soldiers all—and Thomalians

Then—a muffled roar. "The Aradna! The Jarados!"

And there was something else—the Bar was climbing the stairs, leaping forward. Hal Watson watched him swinging his weapon, aim it across the dais. He could feel the effect— a strange sensation of vibration that rose from the center of the stone and ringed about the edge of the Spot.

A curtain of blue flame! The Senestro halted; his hand went up. He plunged through.

But by that time they were across. The queen had spoken to the gorillas. One of them had caught the Bar, hurled him back. The professor touched the golden scroll, pressed against it. They had stepped into a chamber of peace.

XXVII

UNDER THE SPOT

THAT WAS the exact sensation! Peace! The effect was stunning! So much had happened during those few torrid moments Hal Watson was dizzy, his body reeled. And now, all at once, he had stepped into a pool of tranquillity.

Silence—complete, golden!

The professor was standing still; behind him was a light, tri-colored, blinking a mystic significance. The maiden turned about, listened. She knelt down.

"Professor," she said, "I knew the day would come. I have waited. I would save my father's people. Never have I doubted."

It was a touching moment. The old man held out his hands, placed them on her crown of golden hair; he answered:

"Let us hope. God give us strength for these last few hours. Perhaps we can accomplish our task. But that depends upon certain almost impossible conditions."

He was growing stronger each minute; the fire returned to his eyes; his words were firm. First of all, he turned to the mystic lights; gazed back through the walls out at the snow stone. He spoke to Hal Watson:

"We are safe here. This is the secret that has kept me alive during all these years. We are standing within the focus of several dimensions, where lines of force cross. Without this knowledge the Senestros cannot absolutely control the Spot. But come!"

He led the way to the center of the room where a stair led down through walls of gold and silver, winding about in corkscrew fashion to a lower level. There he stopped and felt along the wall, fumbling here and there until he had picked something from a hidden niche—a red stone about the size of a boy's marble.

That done, he walked to the opposite wall where another stone cast a red light across the apartment. Carefully he placed the first one against the second, waiting for a full minute, when a bright glimmer broke out, speading until it revealed a hidden door with a blue metal knob. They had passed through.

This room was different from the others—perfectly round. The walls were a creamy substance, like polished ivory. But the greatest wonder was the ceiling—a vibrating sizzle of metallic energy, seething with magnetism and life.

It was the snow stone itself!

The professor pointed. "Now we have it," he said. "Behold! Here is the center of the Thomalia—the point of contact—the mystery of the ages!"

Hal Watson gazed upward. It was alive, surely enough; suspended in air, whirling softly and yet standing still. At no point did it come in contact with the sides of the room. Then he noticed something else. Notches in three colors— those of the mystic leaf, red, green, and blue, running about the whole of the stone. Stepping closer he perceived that each was a rare gem—of scintillating brilliance. Figuring swiftly, he counted twenty-seven sockets; all of them full. The professor explained:

"Here we have the first secret. And it was here, Hal, that we picked up the first solution of the Blind Spot. Three of those stones were missing on the day of the great judgment years ago. Your father supplied them from the earth side. But that was all we knew. It opened the Spot but did not control it. That was why I never got back to earth. The Spot jammed as you might say. And we were imprisoned."

166

THE SPOT OF LIFE

"But you have learned a lot more since?"

The old man nodded: "A great deal. For six years, until the slaughter of the Rhamdas, I had complete access to this temple, to the hidden chambers, and all the secrets of the sacred books. I was looking after facts—and the scientific explanation of the phenomenon. Some day I planned to return to my own earth, which, after all, is not far distant. For instance, right at this minute you are standing in the house at 288 Chatterton. Our friends are about us. San Francisco? So near and yet so far. But come. We have a great deal to accomplish."

He turned to the ivory wall, traced his fingers along the sides until he had reached a spot directly opposite the door, where he reached up and pressed a hidden depression.

Instantly the walls began receding, transforming from a solid substance into a seemingly vaporish barrier. The room was expanding, the floor lifting along the edges until they were breast high with the snow stone.

Again Hal Watson noticed the rush of magnetism. The great circle of the stone had begun to vibrate in the other direction. The thing was automatic, eerie, silent. Here was Intelligence, some great spirit controlling vast and unseen forces.

The professor had reached out and picked up a tripod—spread it, and placed it under the depression in the wall. Next, he produced a metal clover leaf with an empty socket in each petal. The two instruments went together exactly like a stand and a camera. Hal Watson noticed the tips of the legs set in blue stone; no doubt as an insulation.

Again the professor sought along the wall. This time he worked with the red stone, tracing it along like a magnet, until it fastened itself suddenly to the vaporish partition. Instantly the point of contact began coloring, first into a gray,

167

then a blue, spreading itself into the shape of a circular door. A drawer popped open. The professor glanced up.

"Behold the secret of the Jarados! Had I known of this years ago, we would never have been trapped. These stones"—selecting three scintillating gems from the compartment—"are the keys. Their effect is beyond belief. Yet, they are simply elements—as natural as our own iron or copper. This is the one we shall use."

He returned to the tripod—placed the round black stone in the middle socket. He spoke to Hal Watson:

"Now then, tell me all that has transpired; how you passed through the Spot, everything. Just who was with you, and how long you have been at 288 Chatterton."

Hal related all he knew. The professor considered.

"And Flanning was the only man with you?" he asked. "This all happened during one afternoon and night? Who is this Jimmy Fuillard?"

Again Hal explained. He told about telephoning in the restaurant—how he had given Fuillard's card to the detective.

"Does he know anything about science? Mathematics?"

"I don't think so. But he is a college man. He mentioned the Blind Spot to me once. There was a mathematician with him at the time. His name was Van Tassel—he looked like a dreamer."

"Ah. That is better. A mathematician and a dreamer. It would take a man like that. God grant us this one chance. It is only one in a million. It alone can save us."

The Aradna spoke up.

"Are the odds as great as that? I know about this side. But surely the earth men will be able to protect themselves. My father was a great man. And you—even the Senestro compares you with the Jarados."

The professor smiled.

168

THE SPOT OF LIFE

"You forget, my dear," he said, "that the rank and file of earth men are far below those of the Thomalia. You have had the advantage of two hundred thousand years. That is a long time. Your science is almost unbelievable. For instance, the Senestro with his knowledge of dimensional force could wipe out San Francisco, clean it of all life, in twenty minutes. Once let him land a few high power weapons upon the Chatterton height and the end would be at hand. He would save the buildings, but life would be gone."

The old man had taken on new vigor; he turned to look at the black stone set in the socket. A tiny speck of light shone at the top, infinitesimal, yet manifest. Carefully he studied it, turning it around. He looked up.

"I am getting in touch with the other side. It is the only way. If no one answers, the house at 288 Chatterton will be destroyed. That light," pointing to the stone, "tells of atomic disintegration. On the earth side it will be regarded as a miracle. Once started, it cannot be stopped—except here in the Thomalia."

"What do you mean?" Hal asked.

"Exactly that," came the reply. "Flanning or some one else may see it—first a hole, matter dropping into space. But there will be something else. Even though half of San Francisco should be eaten up, some one will pick out our signal. Now then—"

He reached for the red stone, tapped upon the dot of light. Then he repeated—in code! Nothing happened. He nodded.

"This is one of the times when we must have patience. There are only a few hours left. Outside, the Senestro is marshaling his hosts and instructing his commanders. At the even stroke of the hours the Spot will open. As I say, we have only one chance in a million."

169

THE SPOT OF LIFE

Over in the center of the room the two gorillas were waiting, their bodies weird under the strange light. Now and then they would chatter and snap their teeth. Hal wondered. He stepped over, and looked. For the first time he discovered that the creamy vapor of the moving walls was transparent; at least they could look out. Below them and in front was the concourse of the temple, spreading into the distance. Yet, they themselves were invisible. The two half-beasts kept looking out. The professor explained:

"You are under the snow stone, lost in the cross currents of vibration. Nobody knows of this chamber but myself. It was a secret of the Rhamdic philosophy. The head of the Rhamdas knew—no one else. It is a secret which controls the snow stone. But just how far I do not know."

They had returned to the tripod, where the speck of light had grown larger. It wavered, and began again. Finally, the professor inserted a second jewel in the adjoining socket. It gave off a green color. After several minutes it too began filling with a weird scintillation, flickering for all the world as though it were being tampered with.

"Ah!" the old man leaned forward. "It must be Flanning. Wait a minute. I'll keep calling. Now!"

The light deepened. It stopped, blazed up, died down. The professor tapped another message.

"Our chances are getting better," he spoke to Hal Watson. "If we can only signal through. Hello! What is this?"

His face was almost touching the stone. The lights began to flash suggestively. Over and over, they were repeated. The professor breathed the words:

"Thank God! The miracle has happened. Detective Flanning has done just what you hoped he would do. He went for Jimmy Fuillard, and the latter hunted up Van Tassel. They have got our signal. Now we shall see what we can accomplish."

XXVIII

THE PROFESSOR PAYS

HAL WATSON was befuddled. There was so much to learn, and so little time. It was all like a dream. During the past forty hours he had been shunted into the cross currents of strange dimensions.

Who was at 288 Chatterton, and what was happening? No doubt Flanning had called in the police and others. But what could the officers do against such a thing as the Spot of Life? He spoke to the professor.

"Then we have only a few hours?" he asked. "The Spot will open? How do you know?"

"By the calendar. The Senestros have calculated the periods. They know the day. The clocks tick the hour. Then —the Spot will open, for good."

"For good? What do you mean? Perhaps it will close again."

"Not unless we can stop it," came the reply. "I can do that; but I don't know what will happen." He held the red stone in his hand. "We have the key here. Also it is the talisman to certain things hidden on the earth side. If your friend Van Tassel follows the instructions I have given him, we can go through."

Hal Watson picked up the red jewel, balanced it in his palm. It was shaped like an egg, smooth and polished; but with a sort of negative sensation. It rendered his hand numb and lifeless. The old man nodded.

"You have felt it," he said, "and it has registered. Negative! But just what it is, I cannot tell you. I only know that it is the spark of the snow stone. When the moment comes, you will see. And now here is something else."

171

THE SPOT OF LIFE

He reached into the compartment and pulled out a sheaf of manuscript—a book of strange design; again he explained:

"And we must not forget these. Whatever happens, hang onto them. I may be killed. If I am, do not pay any attention to me. Seize the book. It contains all. On earth it will advance scientific thought many thousands of years. Remember."

The girl stepped forward, held out her hand; she seemed to understand.

"It is the book of the Jarados!" she exclaimed. "The laws of the Thomalia! The scientific explanation of Life. I have heard."

"Life?" Hal Watson spoke the word. His thoughts raced back to the beginning to the weird prophecy of Professor Holcomb. He was going to prove death—lift the screen of the Occult. He repeated the one word—"Life?"

"Exactly," said the professor. "Life and death. The equation of mystery. Death, a dimension. My boy, you have guessed it. For instance—"

"What?"

The old man had turned from the tripod; he held up his bony hand; his eyes snapped with uncanny wisdom.

"You have seen, and still you ask? But that is because you are fundamental; you interpret matter with three dimensions. You are earthly. Five senses hold you in slavery. But," he waved his hand at the tripod. "I have just talked to one who understands—your man Van Tassel."

"Van Tassel?"

"A man and a scholar," announced the professor. "I have sent him word in code. He knows. Mathematics led him through. Beyond the second law of dynamics. Let me explain. Take your chemistry. What happens? Nothing is ever destroyed, is it? Yet there is a mysterious thing in mathe-

172

matics called the quantity H—this law of dynamics. In simple words it is the end—when nature, every atom of matter, loses its energy, and become nothing. Is it not so?"

"Yes, I think I have heard of it."

"Also, there is another law worked out by your mathematics—another variation of this one, which produces a perfect zero. In other words, your universe harmonizes into a circle, of tremendous nothingness."

"Go on," Hal said.

"Well," continued the professor, "it is so. A law reached by means of coefficients. For instance, length, breadth, thickness, time, space, motion, energy, inertia, stress and consciousness. It is a deep problem and understood by few; but the answer is perfection. And that," pointing to the snow stone, "is what you have!"

The earth man was amazed; he spoke.

"Then the Bar Senestro told the truth. This Jarados was a man. A human being like ourselves."

"Absolutely. Every word of the Senestro was a fact. The Jarados—a man! The Rhamdas—a priesthood! The Spot of Life—perfection, therefore a contact! Remember, there is not a thing in the universe from atom to nebula that does not answer the same law. Harmony. Therefore, the Spot of Life may be solved."

Hal Watson was not so sure; he gazed back at the seething circle of mystery, felt its strange vibration. The girl was standing by his side, her hand holding his. She looked up and smiled. And then—another mystery swept through his heart. It was flitting—a zephyr of new-born love. Hal Watson did not know. He only felt and saw.

But just then something happened. The light of the tripod deepened. Over at the edge of the vapor one of the gorillas began acting strangely—a blur passed before them.

173

THE SPOT OF LIFE

The professor turned and tapped a signal. Two gorillas! Then only one!

The other had disappeared.

For a moment! And then the report of a gun! Simultaneously the big beast called Balwa staggered back. He was clutching his arm. A spurt of blood was seeping a crimson stain!

The Aradna leaped forward, caught the monster by the wrist. The big fellow churned and stamped, his teeth clicking a frenzy, while the other danced around. The little queen had become solicitous and tender. Like the beast's, her teeth clicked in an uncouth tongue, chattering with excitement; finally she called to Hal.

"He doesn't know what happened. He only knows that there were men and that one of them pointed a weapon. There was a noise. And then he was back again in this chamber of silence."

Hal examined the wound, found it slight and helped bind it up. However, he had been mighty glad to hear the report of the gun. It was from his own world and it proved that the professor had spoken the truth. He was still in the house of the Blind Spot.

The professor had gone back to the tripod, sitting in front, waiting. The light in the middle socket kept winking; but sent no message. He had become silent, patient, immovable. Hal Watson waited and wondered. In the end he turned to the Aradna. Together they walked back to the vaporish wall whence they could gaze out on the temple.

Surely it was the greatest structure he had ever seen—a place of Titans, half temple, half auditorium, a Karnak in immensity and construction. As far as he could look was that ocean of men, armed, uniformed, prepared. Their numbers were legion—extending into the limitless distance of

174

the far corridors. The ceiling was a cloud—a gray-black suggestion of thunder, held up by immense pillars, twisting spirals that rose like prodigious water-spouts, flaring at the top and bottom to hold the earth and heaven in a welded unity.

It took his breath away; here was a conception beyond the wildest flight of earthly architecture, genius or prophecy—the mind of man spanning the ages with an epic of accomplishment. Whatever the morals of these Thomalians, there was no doubting their civilization. He noted the coloring of red and gold, the silver walls, and far in the distance a vast golden scroll. Just then a hand touched his own. It was the Aradna.

"Isn't it wonderful?" she asked. "And it has stood for ages. Its construction goes back to the dim legends of the past—to the Jarados!"

"And he was a man?"

"So the professor says. But it is hard to convince the Thomalians. They have regarded him as a god so long that the Senestros have had a difficult task in convincing them otherwise. The old Rhamdas let them think as they chose—waiting for the day when we could rise to an altruistic level. The Rhamdas, you know, taught the doctrine of perfection—when we were ready we could go through—not before."

"But where would you go?" Hal Watson asked. "What is your idea of the other world? Your father? What was he?"

She could not answer; her eyes lifted; their glint was ecstatic, shading into tears. She was a maiden of two worlds, a creature to cherish. Her words came in a whisper.

"I have always wanted to know. My father's name was Wendell—Harry Wendell, an earth man. My mother was a queen of Thomalia. And I know so little. It is all so strange and spiritual. But the professor has told me a few things. Your world is younger—a counterpart of this, but it is

175

beautiful. The city you saw from the windows is our Mahovisal. It is coexistent with your San Francisco. Our world
parallels yours. Yet, he says it is all natural—like a board
having two sides. What passes out of your world comes
into ours, and vice versa."

"You mean death?"

"And life," she answered. "We don't like the name of
death. After all, it is only a phase. We live forever."

Hal Watson was watching that tremendous multitude; his
thoughts were not so hopeful. Should the Thomalians ever
pass through to the earth, there would be massacre aplenty.
Death was more than a name. He thought back.

"Why did the Senestro want to get hold of me?" he asked. "What could I tell him?"

"Nothing," came the answer. "But you are the professor's
grandchild. The Bar has his own interpretation of the earth
man's psychology—the man who fears death; through you
he could make the professor talk. But I was prepared for
that."

They were standing close together, their hands touching.
Hal Watson felt a spray of golden hair against his cheek.
But she did not look up. Rather, she was interested in that
concourse of soldiers, far reaching, their faces lifted towards
the throne. But suddenly the multitude stirred, rose to its
feet.

Something had happened!

Simultaneously a vibrating sensation shot from the inner
chamber, followed by a subdued hum, like a motor speeding up. Hal Watson turned, looked at the snow stone. He
leaped back.

The great vibration was changing color, running from snow
white into a strange unholy pink. Along the edges it was
red—fringed with blue flame, the whole mass seething in a
whirlpool of motion. The lighting of the room had deepen-

176

THE SPOT OF LIFE

ed; the air was tense. And over by the ivory vapor was the professor, his wrinkled little face screwed to the dot upon the tripod, watching, waiting. Now and then he consulted a map upon his lap. Hal Watson leaned over—all he could make out was a ten-pointed star and a mass of hieroglyphics. The old man held up a warning hand—asking for silence.

The light in the second socket danced; dots and dashes coming from the void. Then suddenly the third socket lit with a perilous red—deepened into warning. The little old man tapped desperately. He waved his free hand, pointed to the stars.

What could he mean?

There was only one answer. Hal Watson hurried; the Aradna right behind him. Next instant they were at the wall half circling the snow stone dais, looking through the transparency at a pool of vital flame. The whiteness was entirely gone—the pink of the lower side of the Spot had become crimson at the surface—leaping, twisting, torturing itself into a caldron of energy.

What was going on?

And beyond the stone was another picture—the columns of men hurling themselves into the vortex. The rear ranks were shoving those in front, where, at the edge of the Spot, they disappeared like so many moths. The Aradna was fascinated. Hal Watson clutched the wall.

Where were the soldiers going? Had they been consumed by the vibration? And what had become of the Senestro? Down beneath he could distinguish a peculiar hum—such as he had heard in the council chamber—*Haroom! Haroom! Haroom!*

Another thought flashed. Perhaps the column of men was passing through—heading into the house at 288 Chatterton! If that were so, nothing could stop them. The Aradna clutched his arm; she pointed.

177

THE SPOT OF LIFE

Far in the rear, along the golden wall, he could see the many-faced clock, the twenty-four hands working around. All but one was pointed at the spot on the top—twelve; the last hand still lacked several minutes. The queen called in his ear:

"It lacks the time. The Spot will not fail. There! There! Look!"

She was pointing at the Senestro, followed by his Bars obstructing the way to the snow stone. But it was a snow stone no longer; the pool was seething like the atomic caldron of the sun—first a crimson, a violet, a green, then a mottle of boiling iridescence. The column of soldiers had halted.

Again Hal heard that purring beneath the stairway—felt the vibration of the under side. Some one called his name. The Aradna spoke in his ear.

" 'Tis the end! The professor will save us. Perhaps we shall perform the impossible. But come."

Once again they were at the bottom of the stairs, peering through a ring of unaccustomed light. The top side of the stone had gained speed—shooting up the mystery of life. But down here it was not hot—the air was cool, magnetic! Over near the ivory wall was the professor.

But what had happened?

The old man was stooped, shrunken. His bony hand trembled—his voice was weak. And yet, he held to his post. The lights in the tripod flickered again, and again. Hal Watson could see death in the wrinkled features.

Would the professor hold out; and if he didn't, what would happen? All the work of the genius of the Blind Spot would go for nothing. They would be trapped—in the Thomalia! And what was worse, the Senestros would pass through to the defenseless earth.

The old man gasped, fell to the floor. He looked up,

pointed toward the Spot of Life. Came the words:

"I am too late! Help me, Hal! I am dying—dying—of the Blind Spot! It has killed me."

The Aradna was kneeling down; the green light in the socket was blinking banefully. The old man moved his hand; the eyes wandered up and down, plainly they were passing over the border; then his body stiffened in the death spasm—for a flash of a second—only to settle again. The great eyes opened wide and consciousness returned. The wan lips whispered.

"The Spot of Life! In the center—a whole—a socket. The pigeon-egg stone! Red! It—"

That was all; the life and greatness of Professor Holcomb had passed into the shadow. Hal Watson was alone with the mystery of the ages.

XXIX

FLUX

IT WAS A crowded half hour at 288 Chatterton Place.

First of all, the detective called up headquarters. The chief answered. Flanning was crisp, imperative; he asked for a riot squad and machine guns. Action! He got plenty. The heavy cars tore through the city. The chief dashed up the stairs, clamored into the house. But when he stepped into the room he stopped with an exclamation of amazement.

Two men were bending before a queer looking jewel, taking down a message from a light. The thing winked and sputtered. But there was no sign of violence or trouble of any sort, merely the little German waving a warning hand. Flanning was gone.

"Well," snapped the chief, "what's the trouble?"

Just then another car roared up to the door. It was Sam Flanning coming in with a telegrapher. The man Van Tassel had risen; he pointed to the stone.

"Don't ask questions," he said to the chief. "Yust be ready. You'll see enough presently. Get those guns set. Flanning, you take charge. Here is the room. Have the gas bombs ready. As for myself, I have work to do."

That was all. The little fellow darted for the table, picked up the diagram, caught the telegrapher by the arm, led him back. In rapid words, he gave directions.

"Take down the message," he directed. "Every word. Hand it to Couland; he'll pass it on to me. That's all. Don't waste your breath mid foolish questions."

Then with the diagram in his hand, he picked up the

180

library stone, the one he called the accelerator, and began tracing it along the wall, slowly and tenatively until he picked up a magnetic field. Instantly the jewel turned color and gave off. a soft glow, revealing a dot in the partition. The speck grew larger and finally materialized before their eyes—a jade colored substance about a centimeter in diameter. From all appearances it had been embedded for years. But Van Tassel did not touch it. The discovery was enough.

He went on.

This time he consulted his figures, leaving the wall and exploring the deep center of the room. Again there was the same reaction—another dot; only this one, like the messenger stone, was suspended in pure air, its color amethyst until touched by the stone indicator, when it turned to a fleshlike pink. The German nodded his satisfaction.

"*Ja!* Yust like he says. If we find der others we shall know. If—"

Steps sounded in the hall; a motor was purring outside. Two bespectacled, middle aged men of apparent culture entered the room. They stopped at the sight of the officer. Then one of them glanced at the telegrapher. He gasped.

"What is it?" he asked, looking at the suspended stone. "Is this the reason we have been so hastily summoned? The phenomenon—Ah!"

But Fred Van Tassel was not talking; he had turned half around, grasped a paper from Couland. He read it eagerly pointing with his thumb to the telegrapher. Again the scientists gasped; the jewel was winking its mystery in shades of green. It was plain that the man at the board was taking down some sort of message. The police, the guns, the gas bombs completed the setting.

"What is it?" they asked the chief.

181

THE SPOT OF LIFE

"Search me," came the answer. "But it seems to be enough. Can you account for that?" He indicated the green flashing light.

Again the signals spotted, coming fast. The telegrapher crouched low, watching and straining his eyes lest he make a mistake. His face had become pale; the veins stood out on his forehead; his stubby pencil scratching automatically across the paper. Van Tassel darted here and there. Only once did he speak.

"I have no time now, gentlemen." he commented. "But I want you to see and watch. In a few minutes there will be more. Mebbe the end."

After that he became an automaton, hopping about, consulting with the telegrapher, measuring and calculating. The map came into play continually; now and then he marked off a star. And through it all the spectators sat still—the police, the scientists, Doctor Colyer and Jimmy Fuillard; and last, but not least, the uncanny old lady from the neighboring dwelling. She alone broke the spell, her voice droning:

"My, my! This is the work of the devil. I always knew it. And I always said it."

Then silence. The suspense had become magnetic—oppressive; and all the while the chemist continued his search, picking out a network of queer looking elements, which, as soon as he touched them, suddenly became alive. The room began to take on a strange color of weird light; ranged in a circle, the uncovered objects appeared to supplement each other in keyed segments, weaving a peculiar magnetism, one for the other. Finally, the German had come to the tenth stone. He turned to his companions.

"Ah!" he said. "Vat is der time? Tell me—eleven—twelve? What? I have forgotten."

The chief of police consulted a watch.

182

THE SPOT OF LIFE

"It's just exactly four minutes to twelve o'clock," he spoke. "Four minutes lacking midnight. Now—"

He stopped suddenly. From nowhere there came a subdued sound, unholy, and unearthly—*haroom, haroom, haroom!* The thing augmented and passed into the distance, like a subdued earthquake. Simultaneously the ten stones began throwing out a light—diametrically across the circle —ten colors striking at the center and weaving into a white spot of incadescence, which augmented until it had gained the size of a baseball. Then it stood still.

And all the while the telegrapher was performing his task, scratching frantically, to take down the message. But suddenly he stopped, stood up. He passed the paper on to Van Tassel. Something had happened.

Van Tassel read. Read again, clutched at his head.

"*Mein Gott!*" he exclaimed. "For one more minute! Professor Holcomb! He is dying. He can send no more. He says for us to hold out to the end. So it is up to us, gentlemen to fight." He turned to the detective. "Flanning. Are you ready?"

And Flanning was. He pointed at the police, the guns, and the stacks of bombs behind them. The officers were waiting, puzzled, each and all watching the miracle functioning before their eyes. The network of colors streaking across the circle had suddenly grown deeper, twisting into spiraled cords of life and focusing into the white incandescence like so many spokes in a wheel. Slowly the whole thing began to revolve.

One minute to twelve!

Again that sound in the distance—*haroom, haroom, haroom!* This time it was awful—like the approach of doom! The wheel gained momentum—seething in a circle of flame— a plate of magnetism, a caldron of vibrating energy. In the

183

center was that core of incandescence—blinding. Then—Something else!

A blue dot on the ceiling—the bluest color of the spectrum, spiraling, and finally dropping a string of pulsating light into the incandescent core.

The room had opened. The vista of four walls had gone, and with it all suggestion of earthly surroundings. Instantaneous! Immense, titanic, cataclysmic! As far as the eye could reach—a seething multitude. Like the ocean lifting for a tidal wave; it was moving, surging onward towards a silver stairway and a snow white dais.

A throne—a niche out of eternity! The Spot of Life!

And in the center—Hal Watson and a maiden!

The youth was calm, erect, waiting. At his feet lay the body of the dead professor and a book. In front of him, snapping and defiant, paced the two gorillas. The Senestro was rushing for the gleaming throne, followed by the Bars clad in crimson and gold, leading the columns of the Thomalia. The Temple of the Bell stretched in the distance—vast as the storm of thunder—Cyclopean. And far away the mystic face of a golden scroll.

The scene was one never to be forgotten.

Hal Watson had not stirred; he was watching a tremendous clock in the distance—twenty-three hands all marking twelve, and the twenty-fourth just lacking a second. The Bar Senestro had gained the brink of the silver throne. The earth man's hand was lifted. A red object gleaming like a thousand rubies, shone in his fingers. The hand on the clock had ticked the hour.

But just then something happened. Beyond the Spot, rushing up to the silver throne was the host of the Thomalia—sweeping behind the leaders. And the Bar! He had landed like a panther, snapping, on the balls of his feet. The

184

gorillas were heading him off, springing. They flailed their arms. The Bar leaped aside! Something gleamed in his hand—the dimension gun! The gorillas collapsed. Fell dead.

All in the lapse of a second. Hal Watson swung his arm, the red stone cut a streak of crimson flame. The Bar rushed headlong; his right hand grasping that of the earth man.

They were struggling for the rubylike stone! But the frail Aradna seemed to know; she clung to her lover—worked behind, picking the red jewel from his fingers. She was just in time.

The two athletes were fighting to the death. Hal Watson and the Senestro! A battle of Titans—two worlds in confict, a cross between ju-jitsu, catch as catch can, and boxing. The great Bar was rushing in and out like a snake. His fist struck, his body heaved. He was like lightening. Hal Watson was holding towards the center of the snow stone, always on the defensive.

What was his object? Around the edge of the Spot a blue circle was forming, rimming like fire. The girl was watching the clock. Then—a vast sound of sonorous music.

One voluminous stroke!

Instantly the Bar swung, their two bodies went into the air; but when they landed the earth man had got his hold —a good old flying mare—the Bar was thrown in a circle, shooting a tangent down the silver throne.

The girl had stooped. The stone flashed, dropped into the center socket of the Spot of Life. The man and the princess had stepped together, their forms entwined. Earthquake! The world vibrated!

Like the crack of doom!

The Karnakian pillars were breaking, collapsing! The heavens pealed thunder! A flash of lightning tore the firmament. Pandemonium! And in the center—earth man and the

185

THE SPOT OF LIFE

Aradna surrounded by bursting flames. The Spot of Life was disintegrating—disappearing! Then the whole scene vanished. They were back in the room of the Blind Spot. The ten jewels had been burnt out—the air was clean.

Hal Watson was standing before them. The Aradna was by his side; and the body of the dead professor lay at his feet. He spoke:

"Thank the Lord! But where is Flanning? Ah!" The Princess Aradna was still clinging. He spoke again: "It was death! Death? But what do we care. The greatest secret of all lies in the Vestibule of the Infinite—Life! And love!"

He was standing still, gazing into a pair of eyes; white arms had circled his neck—her lips framed the words:

"Your world, Hal, and mine! My father's people! Now I shall know—and love!"

In closing it may be well to give a few words from Van Tassel, Fuillard, and the others (except Hal Watson and the Aradna, who had disappeared):

Van Tassel: In the nature of the case, I would like to give a detailed analysis of the phenomenon known as the Spot of Life. This, of course, is not possible here. I lack the space. However, the reader may figure it out.

Life is not a mere accident. It is matter; in the highest form—subatomic, subelectrical—built up from the underlaws of material coefficients. And by the same token, all matter is life. That is the secret flashed by the great professor. Of the mysterious Jarados, I know no more than what Hal Watson has told me. He was a soul far in advance of our own age.

The Spot, therefore, was a composite—the contact of the coefficients. Once the network was uncovered, the miracle developed. Life—unconscious, everlasting. But not the soul!

Finally, let us consider how little we know—each particle

186

of sand, each atom, contains a myriad of unknown laws. But we are on the threshold of great discoveries—the future is before us, and the world is ours.

In conclusion, those who would like to go into the technicalities of my calculations may continue by acquiring my forthcoming work. It is entitled: "Beyond the End is the Beginning!" An abstraction in pure mathematics.

Professor Connor: Inasmuch as I was one of the men summoned at the last moments, I can't say much. However, I am especially interested in Mr. Van Tassel's theory of dynamics, and the fact of dimensions.

We all know that energy is passing continually. Yet it cannot be destroyed. Wherefore dimensions can easily be a fact. The two worlds must be coexistent—what passes out of one, goes into the other; and vice versa. I agree with Van Tassel that there is much to learn.

Flanning: I'm merely a detective. I have seen enough. But I can say right now that I was mighty pleased to learn that I was right about Hal Watson's father. He was murdered.

Fuillard: I would advise the reader to get Van Tassel's book. I'll wait for it myself. Really, I am going to break into a whole lot of nature's laws. Just beginning to wake up, as you might say. Van has set me to thinking.

J. C. Couland: Leave it to Fred Van Tassel. Mathematics is his middle name. He's like this guy Caesar. He came; he saw; he conquered.

Aunt Selena: Ghosts! Nothing but ghosts! The work of the devil! Nothing else. I always said the house was haunted!